PROLOGUE

The car sped past a playground and I was instantly reminded of that day, eight years ago, when I saw one of them for the first time. Well, two of them, to be exact.

We drove past the playground and some shops, and then the car slowed as we veered onto a ramp to the Garden State Parkway. I was too distracted to take much of anything in – not that the highway was all that scenic, but it was new to me and so I should have been curious. But I couldn't focus. I was remembering that day eight years ago.

I felt her eyes on me before I realised she was there.
I squinted across the fenced-in area, trying to bring

the girl into focus. She seemed to shimmer in the heat. I had never seen her before at my Little Learners School. Her chestnut-brown hair was divided into two tight braids. Braids that tight would have given me a headache, I remember thinking. She wore a plain grey dress and brown shoes. Her dress was longer than the ones the other girls at school wore. It was, in fact, totally unlike any of the dresses I had in my cupboard at home, even the ones I wore for dress-up.

She stood silently, staring at me as I rocked slowly on the rocking horse. The white horse with its flowing, molded-plastic black mane was my horse. All the kids in the fours class knew I never rode the brown horse, only the white one.

I rocked with my pink skirt cascading over the seat and my white trainers with magenta sparkles planted firmly on the footrests. The heat rose in waves off the recycled rubber-tyre shavings on the ground.

I could feel Miss Susie's curious gaze resting on me from the bench near the entrance. I wondered if she knew the new girl's name. She wiped her brow with the back of her hand and remained on the shaded bench, too warm to play with the kids today.

I glanced over at Kendra and Emmy. Their bare legs stuck to the slide and made a squeaking noise as they slid down, one after the other. Noah, Will and Jack played in the sandbox. No one else seemed to notice the girl. She stood by the far edge of the enclosed play space, her eyes on me.

I closed my eyes and rode my horse. Tiny beads of sweat tickled the roots of my sun-kissed hair. Suddenly I didn't feel so good.

My eyes flicked open, and I slowed my rocking. An odd tingling danced across the soles of my feet. Tiny pinpricks of sensation. I took my feet off the footrests, dangling my legs, wiggling my toes inside my trainers. I felt like I might throw up. I opened my mouth to call for Miss Susie . . . and then I saw the girl sitting on the brown rocking horse next to me. She smiled.

I smiled back.

The girl began to rock. I started up my horse too. Side-by-side, we rocked together, our plastic horses keeping time. I glanced back at the other kids. Still no one noticed the new girl. I was glad. I liked her. Maybe she would be my friend. I didn't want bossy Kendra to see her yet. Kendra never wanted to play with me, and she might convince the new girl not to play with me.

The girl grasped her horse's chipped black mane with her right hand, gripping the handlebar with her left. I did the same. The girl nodded at me, and it was clear: Our horses would race. We galloped back and forth, our horses neck and neck. I turned to smile at her and sucked in my breath. The brown horse had no rider.

My new friend was gone. Just like that.

I gnawed my bottom lip, confused. Where did she go? I twirled about, searching the playground. But I didn't see her anywhere.

A wave of intense nausea washed over me. Climbing shakily off the horse, I wondered if I'd be sent home. When Will threw up during circle time a few weeks ago, he had to go home. I was pretty sure my dad was at work, and I wondered if he'd have to leave to come pick me up.

Suddenly a different girl stood beside me. She had long black hair swept back into a shiny blue headband. She wore a pretty white blouse, navy-and-green plaid skirt and tall navy socks that stretched all the way up to her knees. She began to skip around the horses. She waved her hand, beckoning me to join.

I wasn't sure what to do. Suddenly I realised that I no

longer felt sick. Miss Susie sat on the bench, fanning herself with a magazine. She didn't seem to notice this new girl either. Noah looked over at me and waved. But he didn't wave at the new girl. I watched the girl's thick hair bounce as she skipped. I looked over towards Kendra, sure that she would tease the new girl for skipping around like a baby, but Kendra wasn't paying attention. I decided that I wanted to skip too.

Around and around we went. I giggled as she made silly faces at me.

Suddenly the girl with the braids was back, atop the brown horse. She pointed toward the white horse. She wanted me to ride with her again. I stopped skipping and stepped in her direction. Not only did I have one new friend, but I had two!

The black-haired girl was suddenly in front of me. She scrambled onto the white horse. My white horse. The two girls began to ride. I wanted to ride too.

"That's my horse," I said quietly, pleading.

The girls kept rocking.

"That's the horse I always ride," I said, louder this time. "I was on it first."

The girl stared ahead, as if she didn't hear me. Tears

pooled in my eyes, and I swallowed hard. I didn't understand what was happening. Why wouldn't she listen? Why didn't they want to be my friends?

I tried to move towards them but couldn't. My feet felt glued to the ground. I tried to reach for the girls, but I couldn't move my arms. I had the terrible feeling that I was being pressed down under a bunch of pillows. I felt like I couldn't breathe.

Miss Susie raced to my side. She drew me close, anxious to uncover the cause of my tears.

I started to tell her about the two girls.

But they had faded away.

As if they were never really there.

I blinked rapidly, pushing back the memory. I am pretty sure that was the first time. They were the first, but there'd been many others. Girls, boys, old, young. They all came to me and then faded away without saying a word.

I pressed my hand hard against the car window, then pulled it back. The sweaty imprint of my palm smudged the glass. I watched as my handprint quickly evaporated, leaving behind the clear glass.

Was it gone forever? Or was it hidden there somewhere?

I didn't know the answer. Just like I don't know what really happened to those two girls from the playground. But I do know that those girls weren't a dream.

They were real.

CHAPTER 1

"See, it's not so different. Open your window and smell the air," my father instructed as we turned off the highway. He pressed a button somewhere to the left of the steering wheel, and my window rolled down by itself.

I cringed at the thought of what I might see out there and turned my back on the warm, summer breeze cutting through the stale odour of the rental car.

"Do you smell the ocean air, Sara?" my father asked, a little too eagerly. "Just like home. I mean, like California. They smell the same, don't you think?"

I didn't think so. The Atlantic Ocean smelled heavy and thick and salty. The Pacific didn't have a smell, or at least it didn't have one that I could remember.

I stared at my chipped purple nail polish, unwilling

to look out the window, unwilling to inhale more East Coast air. My dad was trying so hard to make me happy. But I had this huge knot in my stomach that just wouldn't go away and I couldn't pretend to be happy, not even for my dad. Not today.

Pressing the automatic window button on my side, I heard the glass close, cocooning us once again in our bubble against the world.

"Do you want to talk about it?" my father asked, for what was probably the hundredth time. His voice was gentle. "Come on, Sara, the move will be good for us."

"How do you know that?" I asked, shifting my gaze from the oblong stain of unknown origin on the grey-blue upholstered seat to the grey faux-leather dashboard. I held tight to the belief that if I didn't look outside, New Jersey wouldn't exist. "I liked California."

My dad ran one hand through his curly brown hair. "You'll like it here, too. Give it time." He turned his attention back to the road through the small town, clogged with late-summer beach traffic.

Discussion over. That was classic Dad. He didn't like to dig too deep, or push too hard. He preferred to wait for me to come to him, which was fine when

I was little, but it's a little more complicated now that I'm twelve.

What I didn't get was why – *now* – were we suddenly diving in and moving across the country to some strange shore town where we knew no one?

Dad said it was his job. But, seriously, although my long blonde hair and blue eyes make a lot of people assume I'm a flake, I'm way smarter than that. New Jersey doesn't need another insurance claims adjuster, no matter how great my dad may be at his job. There was more to it. I just didn't know what.

We drove in silence. A lot of people get freaked out by silence. I don't mind it. Dad and I often hang out together without talking. Dad's not a big sharer of thoughts or feelings. At my old school, the teachers always called me shy because I didn't speak much. I don't think I'm shy. I just realised early on that not everything needs to be vocalised. There's a difference between shy and quiet.

"Our street's coming up," my dad announced. "I'm pretty sure I remember it from last time." He'd flown out last month to meet his new boss and find us a place to live. I'd stayed behind at Aunt Charlotte's house. We didn't visit my dad's younger sister much, and after four days of living with her and my crunchy uncle Dexter on their organic avocado farm, I could see why.

Dad slowed the car, raised his aviator sunglasses, and squinted at the map from the rental counter at the airport. Then he turned right onto Seagate Drive. So my new street was called Seagate Drive. . .

I wrapped my arms around my knees and stole a look out the window. I couldn't help it. My curiosity was too intense.

Old Victorian houses painted pastel colours lined the narrow street. I stared in amazement at a three-story lavender house with powder-blue trim. I'd never seen a house like that before! It was so different from the simple stucco house I'd grown up in.

"Nice street, right?" my dad asked, driving slowly.

"Nice" isn't the word I would have chosen. "What kind of people paint their house pink?" I asked instead, pointing to a pink house on our left.

He let out an exasperated sigh. "Happy people."

I wanted to reply, to say something nice so I didn't sound like such a brat, but the tingling had started. In my left foot. Always my left foot first. *Go away*, I prayed. *Oh, please, go away.* My heart beat rapidly.

I knew what the tingling meant.

Three houses down, a group of dark-haired kids played on a circular white-pebbled driveway. Bikes, skateboards and jump ropes lay scattered about, and shrieking laughter wafted through my closed window. I watched them chase one another, certain they were all related. A girl about my age ran after a younger boy. I wondered what she was like. Then the tingling spread to my right foot and began to creep up my legs.

"Here we are," my dad announced. He waited nervously for my reaction as our car stopped in front of a weathered gabled house.

I blinked several times, struggling to focus. Willing the feeling to go away, I tried to focus on the details of the house. The sea air had weathered the once-vibrant siding. The painted burnt-orange trim was faded and peeling. A huge covered porch with decorative railings wrapped around the front. The second-floor windows opened to several small walk-out balconies. Three large windows protruded from the roof, and an octagonal turret rose along the right side of the house.

The tingling rippled through my entire body.

My dad was saying something about Victorian architecture, but I barely heard him. They were here. I couldn't see them yet, but I could sense them. I knew they were here.

So many of them.

I squeezed my eyes tight, hoping to block them out. Then the nausea came over me, and I felt like I might throw up right there. The force of their presence pushed against me. I could feel them reaching for me . . . needing me.

"Sara? Do you feel all right?"

I opened my eyes and shook my head. "Must have been the aeroplane food," I managed to croak.

"The house needs some work," my dad said. "Except for the little storefront, the house has been totally empty for quite a while. But what do you think?"

My breath caught in my throat as they finally came into view. The old, hunched woman rocking in the swing on the porch. The young man in the cap hanging out the dormer window. The angry-looking man with the moustache by the front door. The slim woman in the long nightgown staring out the bay window. Everyone shimmered and vibrated slightly in the midday sun. My head throbbed.

My father was wrong. The house wasn't empty.

Dead people still lived there.

And I could see them.

CHAPTER 2

The faces shimmered, fading in and out. The man, the woman, the man again. They pulsed like a strobe light, hypnotising me, making me dizzy.

I gathered my strength and wrenched my gaze away, refocusing my energy. I stared at my red Converse trainers. I had doodled daisies along the edges in blue ballpoint pen during science class last year. I stared at the swirling inky lines, memorising the pattern.

"Ready to check it out?" my dad asked, his voice rising with anticipation. I heard him swing open his door.

I wasn't ready. *So many,* I thought. I'd never faced so many. I remained frozen in my seat, my eyes trained on my trainers.

"Sara, come on," my father gently coaxed. "It'll be fine, I promise. You and me, kiddo. Together. That's never going to change, no matter where we sleep. Okay?" He rested his hand gently on my shoulder.

I turned my head and met his gaze. His pale blue eyes twinkled when they locked with mine. "Okay, Daddy-o."

He smiled. It was an old nickname, from years ago. He'd always called me kiddo, so when I was seven I started calling him Daddy-o. I hadn't used it much this past year because he hadn't been around much. Working, I guess, and spending time with his girlfriend, Alexis. Then he'd lost his job, which was hard, and lost Alexis, too, which he thought was hard, but I was secretly glad they broke up. A goldfish had more personality than she did. Maybe Dad and me together again in a new place would be good, I thought.

I pushed open my door and stepped out into New Jersey.

My gaze flickered hesitantly to the house. *Our house.* I exhaled loudly. They were gone. For now, anyway.

Then I stiffened. One remained.

Old and thin, dressed in a gauzy, flowing purple dress, dark hair reaching her shoulders, the woman raised a bony arm and waved. I recoiled as her corpselike arm moved.

Then Dad did the strangest thing. He waved. At her.

I squeezed my eyes to hold back the tidal wave of emotion flooding my body. I wasn't the only one. My dad saw her! He could see the dead people too!

A choked laugh escaped my throat. I couldn't believe it. He saw her!

I see spirits. I have since I was little. Or, at least, now I think they're spirits. In the beginning I wasn't so sure who or what they were. I've never really told anyone about them, even my dad. It's easier not to say anything. If you remain silent, no one judges you or makes fun of you or thinks you're crazy.

I know I'm not crazy.

But I don't know why I can see them.

They've never tried to hurt me or bother me, but they make me feel really sick and scared. At home, I mapped out routes around our neighbourhood to avoid them. It worked, too, but I don't know how I'm going to hide in this town. But if Dad sees them too, then together we—

"That's Lady Azura," my dad said, breaking into my thoughts. "Quite a character, don't you think?"

"Lady Azura?" I repeated slowly. How did he know the spirit's name?

"That's what she calls herself," he explained. "It's for her business. Like a stage name, I'm guessing. She owns the house and lives on the first floor. I've rented the second and third floors for us."

The woman wasn't dead, I realised. She was very old, but very much alive. It'd been too much to hope that Dad could see the spirits too. I was the only one.

"What business?" I asked. I hadn't moved forward and the old woman hadn't stopped waving.

He pointed to a sign hanging in the large bay window on the ground floor. Dark purple letters outlined in a brilliant gold announced: LADY AZURA: PSYCHIC, HEALER, MYSTIC.

"She's a fortune-teller?" My stomach lurched. Seriously? Were we really moving into a house overrun by ghosts that was owned by a fortune-teller?

"So she claims." The skin around his eyes crinkled. He seemed amused.

"D-do you think she has powers? Real powers?" I whispered.

"Sara, don't let that active imagination of yours go into overdrive," he cautioned. He switched to the calming tone he uses when I get anxious. "She's just a nice old woman with a kooky hobby. She won't bother us. I think you'll actually like her a lot once you get to know her. And besides, I can't imagine anyone even hires her. Let's go say hello."

I gazed at Lady Azura again. She was small and frail-looking. In her long, flowing dress she resembled an ancient wood nymph from a book of fairy tales I owned. As I followed my dad up the path and onto the wooden porch, I noticed her wrinkled face was made up heavily. Spiderlike fake eyelashes fanned out from thickly lined lids. Deep crimson lips stood out from the matte powder on her paper-thin skin. Her mahogany hair was obviously dyed. I could see wiry strands of grey creeping in around her hairline.

"Welcome!" she cried. Her voice was huskier and deeper than I'd expected. With bent, arthritic fingers, she grasped my father's hand. "I sensed you would arrive at three, so I came to greet you." She turned her gaze to me. Her brown eyes flickered from my long hair to my navy tank top and jean shorts and down my skinny legs to my trainers. It felt as if she were trying to memorise every detail of my body.

"This is Sara," she declared, then paused, as if thinking. "I can sense your uncertainty. You have a very strong aura, my dear."

My eyes widened as my heartbeat quickened. *What does she know?*

Lady Azura held my gaze, a half-smile playing at the corners of her mouth. Her frail body did not match the determination in her eyes. She radiated strength.

Uncomfortable, I shifted my eyes towards the porch swing. The shimmery outline of an old woman in a dark dress materialised. She sat in the double swing, a pile of yarn in her lap. Her knitting needles moved mechanically as she stared vacantly past me.

"This is all new for Sara," Dad announced. "It's a big change for a California girl. But she's happy to be here, aren't you?" He nudged me.

"Totally," I said. I forced a smile.

"What a beautiful girl you are. The image of your mother," Lady Azura crooned.

I sucked in my breath. "Y-you know about my mother?" She really has powers, I realised.

"I told her," Dad interjected quickly, placing a steady hand on my shoulder. "I showed her a picture of your mum."

"Oh." I relaxed a bit. I never knew my mother. She died right after giving birth to me. Usually talking about her doesn't bother me. Lately, though, I've been thinking about her a lot.

I've seen so many pictures of my mum, and she's honestly the most beautiful woman I've ever seen. My dad once told me that my mum was so pretty that people stared at her all the time. I love being told I look even a little bit like her, and not just because it's a huge compliment about my looks. It makes me feel close to her.

As my father chatted with Lady Azura about house keys and where to park the car, I watched the transparent old woman knit. Her needles moved, but the scarf didn't seem to grow any longer. Then, just as suddenly, she faded away.

" . . . so I'm going to show Sara upstairs and get settled a bit," my dad was saying when I tuned back in.

Leaving Lady Azura on the porch, I followed Dad through the front door and down an entryway painted cranberry red. We climbed a narrow, dark-wood staircase. The carved banister had several broken posts.

The second-floor landing opened into a large room. Browning wallpaper in what was probably once a yellow floral pattern peeled up from the walls. Worn wooden floorboards groaned under our weight. The air was thick and stale. It was obvious no one had been up here for a very long time.

"I know it doesn't look great now, but we're going to fix it up, kiddo." Dad pointed out the floor and ceiling moldings and the walk-out balcony. "This house has character. If you use a little imagination, you can see what a beauty it must have been a hundred years ago."

I didn't have to use my imagination. I could feel it.

This had once been a grand sitting room, a place designed for relaxing. A man with a thick moustache shimmered into view. He read a newspaper in a plush, winged armchair by a roaring fireplace. I could sense he hated to be disturbed, especially when he was absorbed in his paper – because to him, this was *his* home.

"Where's my bedroom?" I asked Dad. I wanted to get away from the man.

"It's up to you," Dad chuckled. "Can you believe we have four bedrooms on this floor and two more on the third floor? I figure we'll put our kitchen table, sofa and TV in this room. We share the kitchen downstairs, but we can always bring our meals upstairs and eat here."

Hallways branched off both the right and left side of the main sitting room. I headed down the right one. "Pick any room you want," Dad said, following me. "I think you'll like this one best." He twisted a glass doorknob, revealing a large room with high ceilings and pale pink walls. A door opened to a lattice-trimmed balcony with partial views of the grey-blue waters of the bay.

I shivered, although it was warm. There was no way I could ever sleep here. I stared at the young woman in the rocking chair in the corner. Her body shook with sadness, and she buried her face in her delicate hands. Her anguish filled my body, causing me to gulp back tears.

"Sara?" My dad peered at me. "Are you okay?"

I backed out of the Room of Sadness, closing the

door on the woman's grief. "It – it's really dusty in there," I explained, wiping my eyes. "I don't like that room. What about the others?"

"You know that we'll clean them, right? Wash away all the grime and dust." He watched me, trying to gauge my mood.

"I know," I said. I tried to smile. I didn't want to worry him.

He swung open the door of a hexagonal bedroom with tall windows and pale blue walls. I could make out the outline of a figure in a sailor's cap by the window. I shook my head. This room was occupied too.

Dad seemed surprised. "You're a picky shopper, I see," he teased. We headed back through the sitting room, and down the other hall.

The bedroom at the end was really cool – octagonal with many windows, all with lace curtains. Although no one appeared, I instantly felt my stomach lurch as if riding a roller coaster. Someone – or someone's energy – lurked in this room. There were more spirits roaming this one house, I realised, than I'd encountered all last year.

"Next," I said, turning to open the other door.

"That one's not really big enough—" my dad started.

The room was much smaller than the others. The walls were painted drab beige and a single, narrow window overlooked the street.

"I was planning to use this one for storage—" he began again.

"I like it," I interrupted. "May I have it?"

"Seriously?"

I nodded. It was empty. Totally empty. And that made it perfect. I've been an only child for twelve years. Sharing a room is not my thing – especially when the other person is dead.

Dad shrugged. "All yours, then, kiddo. The moving van with our stuff should arrive this afternoon."

After we peeked at the two large rooms with turreted windows on the third floor, we heard faint calls for my dad from far below.

Lady Azura had placed a pitcher of iced tea and a plate of cheese and crackers on a rusted wrought-iron table out back. The grass in the narrow yard was overrun by weeds. I slid onto a chair, edging myself away from Lady Azura. Her steely gaze made me jittery.

"I think I may tackle this lawn first," my dad commented, as we passed around the crackers.

"The boy who was helping with the yard hasn't been around in a long while." She shook her head in dismay, obviously annoyed at the boy. "There used to be such pretty petunias out here once."

Dad took a swig of his tea. "Give me some time. I'll get things back to the way they used to be."

He spoke in a light tone, but Lady Azura's brown eyes clouded. "They will never be the same," she replied in a low voice.

"No, they won't." Dad's voice suddenly sounded distant. Sad.

"You can't always control life," she replied, her eyes now searching my father's.

"But we all control our own decisions." My dad met her gaze and held it for a moment. "Sometimes we don't make the *right* ones."

"Some decisions aren't ours to make," she responded softly, looking away.

What's going on? It was as if I'd missed the beginning of the movie. "Huh?" I said.

Dad shook his head, as if suddenly surprised to see

me. "I'm going to help Lady Azura fix up the house," he explained. "It's part of our agreement for living here. I'll use our car to buy groceries, and I'll repair things on the weekends and after work."

"Real estate market is getting hot down here. It'll soon be time to sell the house and cash in." Lady Azura added as she waved a piece of cheese. "But no one wants to pay big money for a dump. And I want big money!"

Dad's going to be working day and night, I realised, if she thinks this decrepit house is going to make her rich!

I nibbled a cracker and thought about what Dad had said. I knew he'd lost his job back home, but he got another one. That's why we were here, right? Did we have money problems? I wondered. Is that why we were living with this wacky woman – so Dad could save money on rent?

Back in California I'd gone to school with a girl whose mum and dad both lost their jobs and couldn't find new ones. Her family ended up moving in with her aunt and uncle. I wasn't friendly with the girl, but I used to hear her complain about it to her friends during homeroom. She had to share a bedroom with her cousin, and apparently her cousin talked in her sleep. I wondered if my dad had some sort of money problems like that girl's family did.

I felt Lady Azura's stare and shook myself out of my thoughts. She was definitely looking at my hands. Was she trying to read my palms or something? I squeezed my fingers into fists.

She grinned, like a cat finally discovering where the mouse lived. "Pretty ring," she said. Her gnarled finger pointed at the braided silver ring I always wore.

"Thanks." I bit my lip. Even if she wasn't trying to read my palm, I decided to avoid her when Dad wasn't around. The way she stared at me – as if she knew me – freaked me out.

CHAPTER 3

"We'll start tomorrow," Lady Azura said to me.

"Excuse me?"

"Oops. I haven't filled Sara in yet." Dad shrugged apologetically. He turned to me. "You'll be helping out Lady Azura too."

"Me?"

"Nick's leaving tomorrow," Lady Azura said, pursing her red lips in annoyance. "All people leave eventually." She stared into the distance. "Not all, maybe."

Why is she speaking in riddles? I wondered. I'm usually not this confused. "Who's Nick?"

"Nick used to help in the afternoons. He checked in on her. He ran errands, that kind of thing," my dad explained. "But he's going away to college soon.

So you're taking over. After school, you'll help Lady Azura. There's a store around the corner where you can buy her little things she may need." Dad nodded encouragingly.

"But—"

"There's a bike in the shed out back," he continued before I could protest. "You can use it to get around. The town's not that big."

"We'll have nice times together," Lady Azura said. It sounded more like a command, though, than a comment. I had just vowed to avoid her, and now it looked as if I'd be spending every afternoon with her!

After we cleared the glasses, Dad went to unpack the car. I started back up the stairs to our rooms and stopped. Suddenly, it was all too much.

The spirits upstairs.

Lady Azura downstairs.

I had to get out.

I told Dad I was going exploring. I grabbed my cell phone and my camera from the car and pulled the red bike from the shed. The bike was a little big for me. It seemed fairly new, though. I wondered if she'd bought it for Nick.

I wobbled a bit at first, but in moments I was pedaling full speed down the driveway.

And that's when I almost hit him.

"Whoa!" A guy in a grey T-shirt leaped out of my way.

I braked quickly. "S-sorry," I stuttered.

"Where you racing to?" he asked. His long brown hair fell over one eye. He was cute and probably about seventeen or eighteen.

I didn't answer. I'd never spoken to a cute older boy before. I didn't know what to say. Plus, I didn't know where I was going.

"Just moved in, huh?"

I nodded and examined my trainers again. I wasn't good in new situations.

"Okay . . . well, have fun." He headed towards the front porch, unconcerned about the mute twelve-year-old who almost plowed him down.

Then I realised that must be Nick.

I cringed and pedaled furiously down Seagate Drive. The kids two houses down were still playing in their front yard. The girl I'd seen earlier now wore enormous, oversize sunglasses. Her long, wavy dark hair reached all the way down her back. She was pitching a red kickball to two younger boys. She spotted me mid-pitch. I saw her raise her hand – to wave, to call me over – I don't know. I didn't slow down. The girl looked really nice, but I just couldn't meet any more new people right now.

At the end of my new street, I turned left onto Ocean Grove Road. The houses were smaller and boxier here. The rectangular yards had yellow gravel instead of grass. One yard had an END-OF-SEASON RENTAL sign. The August sun made the pastel houses look as if they belonged in an ice-cream store.

On the corner, I spotted a green-and-white-striped awning and the sign, ELBER'S CONVENIENCE STORE. Two girls in bikini tops and cutoff shorts pushed open the door, blue Slushies in their hands.

I turned onto Beach Drive, which seemed to be the main street. I biked past a sandwich shop, ice-cream parlour, bagel store and three places selling Jersey Shore T-shirts, key chains and plastic beach shovels and pails. Several gift stores and seafood restaurants were tucked between the tourist shops. I wove around families lugging coolers, beach chairs and sandy toddlers.

Beach Drive, I realised, ran parallel to the beach. A couple of blocks down, I turned right and biked under a huge arched sign proclaiming: STELLAMAR BOARDWALK.

The boardwalk buzzed with elderly people in floppy hats, kids on bikes and families. Food stands with colourful signs boasting the best pizza, the best Philly cheesesteak, the best fried clams and the best soft custard lined the weathered-grey planks. The aroma of sausage and peppers mingled with the salty ocean air. Vendors hawked T-shirts and encouraged visitors to play Skee-Ball at the arcade. Over the metal railing, the steely grey Atlantic Ocean stretched to the horizon. Below the boardwalk, the crowded beach was dotted with lifeguard stands and colourful towels. Farther down, a small red-and-white lighthouse rose from a rocky jetty.

"Hermit crab races!" a man by a booth called to me. "Buy a crab and join the race!" He held up a small hermit crab hiding inside a neon-pink shell.

I shook my head and pedalled on.

A pier jutted off the boardwalk forming a *T*. I parked my bike in a nearby rack and began to walk. Pulling my digital camera from my shorts pocket, I surveyed the activity through the lens. The small pier held more food stands, plus games of chance, several rides and a Ferris wheel.

I snapped a panoramic photo of a row of colourful stuffed monkeys at the softball-toss booth, then a close-up shot of pink crystallized sugar at the candy floss stand. I had got really into photography this year, but I only took photos of objects. Never people.

I sat on a bench and felt a trickle of sweat glide down my neck. Pulling an elastic from my wrist, I gathered my hair into a high ponytail. I wasn't used to the East Coast stickiness. The air thickened around me. I felt heaviness on all sides. I couldn't see them, but I could sense them. This was much more than humidity.

The dead were everywhere in this old town.

I forced myself to focus on something else. I snapped several shots of ice cream melting in a paper bowl alongside a rubbish bin.

"Are you really taking pictures of rubbish?" someone suddenly asked from behind me.

I whirled around, startled.

A boy, a few years older, watched me from the

ticket stand of a haunted house. My eyes widened. I hadn't realised that I was sitting directly in front of a haunted house. I hate haunted houses. For obvious reasons.

"The rubbish?" the boy said again. He wore a black baseball cap that had MIDNIGHT MANOR – YOUR SCREAM AT THE BEACH embroidered in green. "What are you going to do with those photos?"

"I make collages," I said softly.

"Collages? Really?"

I hesitated. I wasn't big on talking to people I didn't know. Remember what I said before about being quiet but not shy? Well, maybe I'm a little shy sometimes. He looked nice enough – brown curly hair, greenish eyes, very tan – but still . . .

He reached under the rickety stand and pulled out a serious-looking camera, complete with a zoom lens. Way more advanced than my pocket-size digital. "I take photographs too," he explained. "So the rubbish photo . . . what are you going to do with it?" He sounded genuinely interested, if a bit amused.

"I'll probably go into it on Photoshop on my computer. Change the colour of the ice cream.

Maybe make it rainbow-striped to contrast with the sun-bleached planks of the boardwalk." The words tumbled out as I explained. I loved manipulating images. Changing reality.

"That's kind of a cheat, don't you think?" he asked. "I don't believe in doctoring photos. I show things the way they are. I photograph nature. Fish, shells, the dunes, seagulls—"

Two young boys pulled their dad to the stand to buy tickets, abruptly ending his rant.

I wanted to tell him I *didn't* think I was cheating. It was art. Or, at least, I hoped it was.

My mum had been an artist – and a photographer.

I have photos she took – amazing images where she played with the lighting to create powerful moods. My favourite photo of hers is of a little porcelain angel figurine. It's so simple, but so beautiful. It hung over my bed in our old house. I was going to hang it here, too, in my new bedroom.

"You want to go in?" the boy called to me. "Totally slow today. By the end of the summer, everyone's over it." He shrugged. "I'm kind of over it too. The job, I mean."

"No thanks." I'd never been inside a haunted house before. I saw enough scary stuff on a normal day. I couldn't imagine what I'd encounter in there.

I raised my camera and focused on an empty salt-water taffy box overflowing with crumpled wrappers. I snapped from several angles.

"More rubbish, huh?" the boy called.

I glanced back at him. He leaned on the ticket stand and pressed a large button. Several bars of a foreboding melody blared from a nearby loudspeaker. Why was he talking to me? I wondered. As if he could read my mind, he kept talking.

"Look, I'm bored, okay? I'd quit, but I need the money. I'm saving for a new Nikon." He adjusted the brim of his cap. "You on holiday?"

"Nope. We just moved here."

He raised his eyebrows. "Cool. I'm David. I'll be in ninth grade."

"Sara. Seventh."

"You should totally check out the haunted house. It may look run-down, but it's still way scary. It's a must-see for all the kids who live here!"

"No thanks."

"You chicken?" he teased.

I shrugged. "Just not interested."

"It's real, you know," he said. "This house was haunted first, *then* it became an attraction."

That got my attention.

"In the early 1900s, a ship captain built this house for his young bride. Back then, this house rested on the bluffs, past the lighthouse. Anyway, the captain loved his wife, and they were very happy until"— David paused—"until the night of the big storm."

"What happened?" I couldn't believe I was asking.

"The ship was due back on a Friday, which happened to be the captain and his wife's first wedding anniversary. The wife had prepared a celebratory dinner. She'd set the table. She'd baked a cake. She dressed in her finest dress and waited for her love's return from the sea. Oops, hang on." David stopped to sell tickets and usher the visitors into the attraction.

As I waited, the spots slowly appeared. Dots of light danced before my eyes. A swirling that made me light-headed. I tried to breathe slowly. My stomach swayed and I felt slightly off-balance. I hoped I was just thirsty from the heat.

I *prayed* I was just thirsty.

"But, as I said, there was a storm," David continued. I tried to focus on his words. "Howling winds. Slashing rain. The wife lit all the lanterns in the house, hoping the warm glow would guide her husband home."

David leaned over the stand. The speckled lights faded, but the tingling in my foot started. I bit my lip, bracing for what would come next.

"But the ship never returned," he said. "The wife sat in her pretty dress by the window overlooking the sea and waited and waited. She didn't eat, even though the feast and cake were set out on the table. She didn't sleep."

A hazy glow glimmered alongside David. Dull at first, but growing in intensity. I shifted and slid to the far side of the bench, trying to get away.

"Hey, don't you want to hear the end of the story?" David asked.

"The sun," I said, as if that were an explanation. "Go on." Twisting back around, I forced myself to concentrate on David's face as he spoke. *Focus on details like you're taking a picture,* I told myself.

"She was found withered and dead weeks later in that very spot," he was saying.

"Horrible," I muttered. Pushing out this one word was a challenge. The glow had gained form, and the pressure around me deepened. I began to see the outline of a man.

"But she never left the house. Not really. The following owners reported seeing lights flash and seeing a woman standing by the window. . ."

The man seemed old. Stooped over. Shaky.

"The guy who built the pier had the house moved here." David gestured to the Victorian mansion behind him, but I was transfixed by the man – who was now moving *towards me*.

I recoiled, nearly falling backwards off the bench.

"Whoa! It's not that scary," David said. He laughed.

I couldn't respond. My eyes expanded in fear. The man kept moving forward. Moving towards me. Never before had a spirit advanced on me. They just shimmered and kept their distance, as if we were divided by an invisible barrier. The living on one side, the dead on the other.

The old man was only inches away.

His eyes, not vacant like all the others I'd seen before, focused upon me. No longer was there a barrier. It was me . . . and him.

And then I felt his deathly cold grip on my bare shoulder.

CHAPTER 4

I screamed as the icy hand squeezed my shoulder.

"Did he really scare you?"

I whirled about. The girl with the oversize sunglasses from my street stood behind me. Her hand rested on my shoulder. She held an enormous Slushie in her other hand.

"You're shaking." She removed her hand and took an exaggerated slurp of her drink. Frosty red liquid shot up the wide straw. "You okay?" She looked genuinely concerned.

I scanned the boardwalk, trying to get my bearings. He's gone, I realised. The spirit of the old man had vanished.

"I'm good." I wasn't really, but there was no way I could explain.

David handed a woman in a floppy sun hat a ticket. He pressed the music button, and the haunting melody played as she entered the mansion's double doors. "Wow! You were totally scared," he said, pleased with himself.

"Yeah. I was." *Just not by you,* I thought. I took a deep breath.

"Oh, get over yourself, David!" the girl cried. "You're about as scary as an after-school cartoon." She turned to me. "Do not let this boy play with your mind."

She gave him a playful shove, then twisted back to me. "So how's your first day here? I saw you before. Speeding down our street like someone was chasing you. My cousin Nick came by and said you seemed upset, so my mum sent me to go hunt you down. She's big on making sure everyone in a ten-mile radius is happy. So here I am." She raised her sunglasses and peered at David. "Personally, I wouldn't have chosen my cousin here to cheer you up. I would never call Nature Boy cheery."

"I'm cheery except when you're around, Lily," he countered. His smile betrayed him. He was teasing her.

"You're cousins?" I repeated, looking back and forth between them.

"I know! Can you believe David and I are related? I mean, Nick – you met him, right? – he's a total cutie, so that makes sense that we share blood. He's my cousin too. But David here" – she took a rare breath while speaking – "definitely problems on that branch of our family tree."

She didn't give me a chance to respond. Not that I had any idea what to say.

"Oh, wow. I never introduced myself. My mum is always on me about my manners. I'm Lily Randazzo. I'm twelve too. Nick told me you're twelve." Lily's chocolate-brown eyes danced as she talked. She wore white cutoffs and three long silver necklaces over an electric-blue tank top that seemed lifeless compared with her personality.

"I'm Sara Collins," I said. "I—"

Lily grabbed my hand before I could finish and pulled me off the bench. Her fingers were still cold from the Slushie. "Let's walk. Nick told me you're from California. Do you know any movie stars? Oh, you look like such a California girl. I would die for your amazing blonde hair. Is everyone as gorgeous as you out there?"

I followed Lily, wondering how Nick had managed to scrounge up so much information about me. My dad was pretty quiet. I didn't see him gossiping with some random college boy, but it had to have been him. Surely, Lady Azura wouldn't have talked so much about me. . .

Lily bubbled on about Stellamar, and I told her about California. She was disappointed to discover that I didn't live near Hollywood and had never seen a celebrity, but she quickly found other things about California to exclaim over. She seemed to see the bright side in everything. Her energy was contagious.

"I'm so glad you moved to our street. I have three brothers, and Cammie, that's my little sister, is only four, so I could so use a girl nearby."

"Me too." And, strangely enough, I *was* glad that Lily was my neighbour. I wanted to be friends with her. Real friends.

I'd never had a best friend. I'd always kept to myself because it's hard to truthfully answer questions about why I get dizzy and act weird sometimes. I gazed at

Lily, who was showing me the dance moves of the jazz routine she performed at a recital last spring. People gazed curiously at her, but she didn't care. She danced on.

I really liked her.

I sprawled on my teal and raspberry duvet in my new bedroom two days later, scrolling through the photos I'd taken so far. Yesterday, Dad and I had walked the length of the beach together. I'd snapped a kid's sand castle disintegrating as the waves crashed down. I couldn't wait to download it onto my computer. Maybe begin a new collage.

I eyed the boxes piled by my dresser and groaned. My computer was packed away in the largest box. Dad had promised we could bring my computer and art supplies upstairs to the third floor and convert one room up there into a craft room. But today was his first day at the new job. I had no idea what time he'd be home.

I thought about dragging the boxes upstairs myself, but then dismissed the idea. I didn't know who was lurking up there – and I didn't want to find out. The spirits in the house had left me alone so far.

"Sara! Sara!" Lady Azura's husky voice floated up the stairs. For such a frail woman, she packed extraordinary lung power. "Sara! Could you come down?"

I headed downstairs, feeling a little apprehensive. It was our first time alone together.

Except I couldn't find her.

She wasn't in the foyer, or the sitting room with its overstuffed sofa and chairs, or the kitchen directly behind the sitting room. A deep purple crushed-velvet curtain hung across the doorway to the right of the front door, opposite the sitting room. I hesitated.

"What are you waiting for, child?" Lady Azura called. "Come in."

How does she know I'm here? I wondered.

Pushing the thick material aside, I stepped inside.

A round table with a silky red tablecloth and gold-lace overlay stood in the centre of the room. An enormous crystal ball on a pedestal and a fanned-out deck of tarot cards rested on the table. A huge armchair covered in a nubby mustard fabric and two spindly wooden chairs were gathered around. An ornate woven tapestry depicting the moon, the planets and the stars hung on the side wall. Thick red curtains held back by braided gold rope shaded the front bay windows. Dusty leather books, crystals and mysterious-looking containers of colourful liquids filled the shelves lining the back wall.

It's the perfect fortune-telling room, I realised. The air radiated with expectation and hope.

"Hello?" I called uncertainly. A small, fringed lamp on a corner table and eight candles of various sizes all smelling of cinnamon gave off dim light.

"Back here, dear," Lady Azura called from behind another purple velvet curtain in the back corner.

It's like searching for Oz, I thought with a smile. I pushed back the curtain and entered Lady Azura's bedroom.

It was like entering a different world.

Everything was white and black. A low-backed sofa in white leather. A sleek glass coffee table. Two modern black chairs with white pillows. A simple bed with stark white bedding. Lady Azura sat at a black-lacquered vanity and stared into a huge mirror surrounded by dozens of round lightbulbs. It looked as if it belonged in an old-time Hollywood dressing room. It was the most sophisticated-looking room I had ever seen.

I watched her shaky hand outline her thin lips with crimson lipstick.

"Ah, you arrive," she said, her attention still on her lips. She added a second coat. Then she turned towards me. "What do you think of my old house?"

I wasn't sure what to say. *It needs a lot of work?* "It's nice," I replied, twisting a strand of hair around my finger.

"You crowded up there?" She stared at me. Her false eyelashes never blinked.

Can she see the dead people roaming about too? I paused.

Lady Azura began to chuckle. A low rumble from deep in her throat. "Oh, my! How could you and your father be crowded in all those rooms upstairs? You must know I'm joking, child." She threw her head back and laughed. "It's so nice to have company after all this time."

I forced out a laugh, as if I'd been in on the joke all along. It was just my imagination. *She doesn't know anything about you,* I reminded myself.

Lady Azura stood. She was a bit shorter than I was. She reached for a silky white scarf hanging on a nearby rack and wrapped it about her head, creating a somewhat modern turban. "So you can ride that bike all right?" she asked suddenly.

"No problem," I assured her.

"Good. I have a list then." She plucked a scrap of paper from her vanity and handed it to me. "Will you be a dear and pick up these items for me? At Elber's and the other stores in town, we have an arrangement. Just give my name, and they'll bill me."

"Sure." I glanced down at the list. Each item was written in her very neat script.

Peppermint Tea
Epsom Salt
Bay Leaves
Gummy Worms (not the sour kind)

"You want sweets?" I blurted.

"I believe in a healthy amount of sugar every day," Lady Azura replied, her tone serious. "I find it balances out the misery in the world." Then she grinned and whispered, "I just love chewy sweets, don't you?"

Suddenly she reached for my right hand, the one without the list. Very gently, she traced the lines on my open palm with her crooked finger. Her eyes peered intently at my palm. For a moment, the only sound was our breathing. Hers soft and controlled. Mine more rapid.

She swayed slightly as she continued tracing. "Mmmmm," she murmured.

"Yes?" I asked, unable to hide my curiosity. Did she know if I'd live a long life? Marry a cute guy? Have tons of kids?

"It's hard to see what others can't, isn't it, my dear?" she asked softly.

I jerked my hand away from her. My heart thudded as I gaped at the fortune-teller.

How does she know?

CHAPTER 5

Before I could ask, the doorbell chimed.

"Ah, my client has arrived." Lady Azura straightened her head scarf and shook out her long, crinkled black skirt. Then she headed through the curtain and across the fortune-telling room. I trailed behind, slightly in awe. I'd never met anyone who could sense things about me – things I'd worked so hard to hide.

She paused in the foyer. "You have my list?"

I held it up and nodded. She reached her hand out, grazing my arm.

I shirked away, still unnerved by her touch.

She opened her mouth as if to say something, but the doorbell chimed twice more. "It's hot outside. Buy yourself an ice cream and put it on my charge," she offered before opening the door.

"Welcome, Mrs McHugh." Lady Azura ushered in a middle-aged woman with short black hair. She wore a pale yellow cotton jumper that strained across her wide middle and black trousers. Her sunken eyes peered about searchingly. "I am so glad Mrs Christie recommended me to you. Please, come in." Lady Azura grasped both of Mrs McHugh's hands in hers and gently led her through the purple velvet curtain. I turned to leave but then paused.

I stood alone in the red foyer, twisting the scrap of paper in my hands. I'd never seen a fortune-teller at work. Lady Azura's raspy voice and Mrs McHugh's nasal drawl were hard to make out this far from the curtain. I tiptoed closer.

Just one little look, I told myself. *Then I'll go to the store.*

Peering through a gap in the fabric, I saw Mrs McHugh sitting at the round table. Lady Azura had plugged an electric teapot into the wall and set it on a hot plate on the table. She perched on the edge of the armchair, directly across from Mrs McHugh.

"Please select a handful of leaves." Lady Azura pushed a white china saucer piled with loose tea leaves towards her client. "Ahh . . . you must choose with your mind, not your hands," she instructed.

She opened the lid of the teapot and motioned for Mrs McHugh to drop the leaves inside. After replacing the lid, Lady Azura reached across the table for Mrs McHugh's hands. "Close your eyes. Empty your mind."

Lady Azura hummed and swayed until the teapot whistled. Then she poured the brewed tea into a large white china cup and placed it before Mrs McHugh. "Let the steam wash over you," she intoned. "Breathe in the scent. Draw it to you."

I watched Mrs McHugh's wide shoulders rise as she inhaled.

"Now, slowly sip the tea," Lady Azura instructed. "Block out all thoughts as you drink. It is just you and the tea. Focus on the tea."

Mrs McHugh seemed deeply connected to the liquid as she drank. Lady Azura reached for the cup. "Now we swirl the tea. Once . . . twice . . . thrice." She pulled a second saucer close and poured the remaining liquid into it. "Ahhh . . . now the tea leaves remain. Their patterns are the patterns of your life."

Both women peered into the cup. I leaned forward to see what they saw, but I was too far away.

"What will happen to me?" Mrs McHugh asked.

Lady Azura squinted into the cup. "I see a bell shape. This bell is a call to attention. And by the bell the leaves form a cat. This cat symbolises an untrustworthy friend. Do you have a friend you are unsure about?"

"Well, lately MaryEllen at work has been acting a little strange—"

"Yes, yes. MaryEllen is one to watch. Be wary of her," Lady Azura warned. "I see wings. Wings tell me you may be limiting yourself at your job—"

"Well, there was a promotion I was going to apply for, but then—"

"You must not put up barriers," Lady Azura interrupted her. "See this fence shape? You are holding yourself back. Do you feel that way?"

"Well, sometimes . . ."

"You need to set yourself free, and then you will succeed at work." Lady Azura peered closer at the leaves. "I see a palm tree here near the bottom. You shall go on a trip soon. A holiday."

Mrs McHugh brightened. "Really?"

"Yes." Lady Azura pointed into the cup. "And see this wagon shape near the palm tree? You will go on the holiday with a childhood friend . . . wait, no, you shall meet your childhood friend *while* on holiday."

"Sonya? Sonya will be there?" Mrs McHugh sounded delighted.

Lady Azura looked up at her client. "Yes, I think it is indeed Sonya," she said in a dramatic voice.

I wrinkled my nose. I bet I could just as easily read this woman's fortune from a pack of M&Ms! Red – you'll find love. Yellow – something scary will happen. . . I stepped away from the curtain, about to leave.

Then I heard Mrs McHugh say, "I'm here because my friend, well, she said that you can reach beyond. She said you can . . . contact the dead."

I froze.

"There is someone you want to communicate with?" Lady Azura asked.

"Yes." Mrs McHugh choked back a sob. "My brother, Ronald. He passed last year."

"Let us begin," Lady Azura said.

I crept back to my spot by the curtain and peered back inside. The lamp had been switched off and the drapes drawn, leaving the room nearly dark. A large white cylindrical candle flickered in the centre of the round table. Lady Azura and Mrs McHugh grasped hands. My throat felt dry. I licked my lips. *Can she really do this?*

Lady Azura reached down by her feet and lifted a large cut-crystal bell. She shook it gently four times. Each time she directed the tinkling bell to a different corner of the room. "We wish to communicate with Ronald—"

"Ronald Amato," Mrs McHugh supplied.

"Ronald Amato, dear brother of Lynn," Lady Azura continued in a monotone. "Move among us, Ronald. Come to us from the four corners of the Earth."

Lady Azura stared straight ahead. Even in the shadowy candlelight, I could see her eyes were no longer focused. "Beloved Ronald, we ask that you join us." She began to sway and hum.

"Ronald . . . Ronald . . ." She chanted his name over and over.

Then the table began to shake. Ever so slightly at first. A small tremor. But then it happened again. And again, until it was clear that the table was moving on its own.

Mrs McHugh's eyes flew open. Her hands still

grasped Lady Azura's. Lady Azura gazed blankly into the distance, as if present only in body and not in mind. I was totally freaked out for a moment before I realised what *I* was feeling: that pins-and-needles feeling had started. A familiar, prickly sensation crept along my skin. The muscles in my throat constricted. I wheezed softly, trying to suck in air.

"Is – is he here?" Mrs McHugh whispered.

The table stopped shaking. I knew the answer before Lady Azura spoke.

"Ronald is with us."

Crouched outside the room, I stared through the break in the curtain at the translucent form of a heavy, bald man in an ill-fitting suit. *Ronald.* He shimmered in the right corner behind Lady Azura.

How did she do it? I wondered. Sure, I could see spirits, but only when they chose to show themselves. I couldn't just make them appear.

"Ronnie, oh, dear Ronnie." Tears streamed down Mrs McHugh's cheeks.

"Ronald, we thank you for joining us," Lady Azura said, her voice low. "How have you been?"

She paused and turned her gaze to the left corner

of the room, behind Mrs McHugh. "Ah . . . he misses you . . . very much."

"Oh, Ronnie, I miss you so dearly." Mrs McHugh tried unsuccessfully to control her sobs. "Please, can you ask him what happened the day of the car accident?"

Lady Azura nodded. "What happened on the day of the accident?" Once again, she directed her question to the opposite corner from where Ronald's spirit hovered. I couldn't figure it out. Why wasn't she talking *to* him?

I'm sorry, Lynnie . . . I should have never tried to make that phone call . . . it was dark and raining . . . should've been watching the road . . . took my hands off the wheel, Ronald replied.

"He says it wasn't his fault," Lady Azura told Mrs McHugh.

The woman raised her head. "Oh, I'm so glad. I knew it couldn't have been his fault he swerved off the road. So he didn't mean to run over the cows?"

"Cows?" Lady Azura seemed confused for a moment. She gazed intently into the empty left corner.

Doesn't she see him? I wondered.

Ooooh, Lynnie . . . I saw the cows . . . like shadows along the road . . . I swerved to avoid the car to my left . . . I made a choice . . . rammed into them . . . but then the car spun . . . Ronald let out a wail of regret, his words fading in and out as he relived the night of his death.

Lady Azura continued to stare into the wrong corner. "He says he never saw the cows until it was too late. He is leaving us now, but he says he is at peace." She dropped Mrs McHugh's hands and heaved a huge sigh, as if drained. "He's gone."

She was right about one thing. Ronnie had left.

She's a fake, I thought, holding back a giggle. Suddenly I found the séance funny. She totally made the whole thing up. She couldn't see or hear Ronald.

Then the realisation washed over me. I pressed my fingernails into my palms.

Lady Azura hadn't heard one word that spirit said. But *I* had.

CHAPTER 6

His voice. I'd heard his voice.

I replayed the séance in my mind. I had seen Ronald – and heard him *speaking*. Questions whirled about my brain. I'd been seeing spirits since I was in preschool. But never – *never* – had I heard one speak. Not to me. Not to anyone. I hadn't even considered that they could speak. I just assumed they couldn't.

Footsteps shuffled in my direction. The purple fabric, separating me from Lady Azura and Mrs McHugh, fluttered. I pushed open the front door. I grabbed my bike from the bottom of the porch stairs and pedalled onto the street.

Why was I hearing them now? Was it only Ronald I could hear? Or could I suddenly hear all of them? The idea made me shudder. Fear tightened its fingers around me, squeezing my ribs.

"Sara! Hey, Sara!"

I turned to see Lily, standing by a row of periwinkle hydrangea plants, wildly waving both arms as if guiding a small plane in for landing. She wore a navy-and-white-checked sundress and her hair fell in two loose braids. A dark-haired woman crouched alongside her, pulling weeds. A little girl dug nearby with a small plastic shovel and sang an off-key version of "You Are My Sunshine." Two boys played tag on the lawn.

But my brain was still puzzling over the séance.

"Hey, Sara! Where you going?" Lily called to me.

I stopped my bike and hesitated. The leap from Mrs McHugh's dead brother to this joyful family was enormous.

"You're it!" The older of the two boys suddenly slapped my bare arm then raced across the yard.

"Go! Go get him!" cried his younger brother. Both boys had thick ebony hair and elfin features. "Run!" He tugged my hand.

I jumped off my bike and sped after the older boy, still holding the younger boy's sweaty hand. Both boys shrieked with laughter as we darted around the yard. It wasn't hard to tag him. "Gotcha!" I cried.

"Again! Again!" cried the younger boy.

"Later, Jake." Lily appeared by my side. "Mum told you and Joey to go inside and have some juice. Sam's in there." She intertwined her fingers with mine and pulled me away from her brothers. "I was wondering when I'd see you again. I wanted to come by, but my mum said it was rude to barge in. She said you needed time to settle. Are you settled yet?"

"I guess." I smiled. Lily's energy warmed even the thick summer air.

The woman behind Lily stood and brushed dirt from her jeans. I knew she was Lily's mum. They looked liked clones. "Hi," she said simply. Her open gaze enveloped me like a hug. "I'm Beth Randazzo. You don't happen to know anything about soil acidity, do you?"

I shook my head. "Never even heard of it."

"The people at the plant store say that's the problem with the hydrangeas to the right of the door. Not enough acid in the soil, so no blooms. But what am I supposed to do?" She raised her hands in mock surrender.

"We could pour orange juice or lemonade on them," Lily suggested eagerly. "Those are acidic."

Mrs Randazzo's eyes brightened. "We could have a lemonade stand this afternoon, then toss the extra there." She turned to the little girl on the ground. "Cammie, want to do a lemonade stand with Mummy?"

"Yes!" Cammie cried.

"Lemonade stand, girls?" she asked us.

"I can't. I have to go to the store," I said apologetically.

"That's right." Mrs Randazzo flushed. "Your family must be so busy, moving in and all. I wanted to be one of those women who brings a pie the first day. I thought about it too. I just wish I knew how to make a good pie. Please apologise for me. Tell your mother I'll come by tomorrow."

"She's not here." I paused. "She died a long time ago. I live with my dad."

Awkward silence. It always happens. People don't know how to react when I tell them about my mum.

"I'm so sorry—"

"It's fine," I interrupted. "I never knew her." When I say that, it makes people feel better. Like you can't miss what you never had. But watching

Mrs Randazzo and Lily, I did miss her. A lot.

"It's not fine," Mrs Randazzo said. "Sometimes a candle is blown out before it even begins to burn. Right?"

"Right." I stared at the wicker basket of cut hydrangeas at my feet. The perfumed scent of the pom-poms drifted towards me. I wanted to reach out and touch Lily's mum. She understood. Very few did. But I kept my hands by my sides.

"Wait," Lily said. "Does that fortune-teller woman live with you and your dad? Is she still there?"

"Yeah. Do you know her?"

Lily shook her head. "My friends are always daring me to go in there, but she seems too wacky. Is she totally wacky?"

"I'm not sure," I admitted. I turned to Mrs Randazzo, who was now gathering the cut flowers into a bouquet. "Do you know Lady Azura?"

"Yes. I love the long emerald-green coat she wears in the winter." She gave a quiet laugh. "The woman's eighty, yet manages to make me feel frumpy."

"But what do you know *about her*?" I pressed. Suddenly it seemed vitally important that I uncover if she was a fake or if she truly had powers. "She speaks in riddles. Do you think her fortune-telling is for real?"

Lily's mum reached for a piece of twine and twisted it around the stems. She seemed to be considering my question as she worked. She took her time, binding the flowers into a puffy, beach ball–like bouquet.

"It's hard to say, Sara," she finally replied. "I suspect that everything she tells her clients is both true and untrue. We can each uncover what's true if we are willing to look for it. There's often a truth that's deeper than the words we hear."

A few minutes later, I biked alongside Lily, thinking about what her mother had said. Was there something about Lady Azura I wasn't seeing?

We made a quick pit stop at Elber's, so I could pick up the items on Lady Azura's list, and then hopped back on our bikes.

"We need to stop at visitor's info," Lily said as we pedalled onto the boardwalk. "Great-Aunt Ro works there. She likes to keep fresh flowers on her desk. These are for her." Lily held the bouquet in one hand and used the other to steer. "You hungry?

Uncle Lenny will give us slices." She pointed the bouquet towards Lenny's Pizzeria.

"Is everyone on the boardwalk related to you?" I asked.

Lily pointed to an older man in a Speedo suit sunning himself on a bench. "Not him, thank god," she replied, and we both cracked up. "But everyone else, probably."

"Really?" With the exception of my dad's sister, we didn't have any close family.

"The Randazzos and the Morellis – that's my mum's side – pretty much run Stellamar and the towns nearby. They've been living here for over a hundred years. And everyone has lots of kids." Lily rolled her eyes. "I mean *lots*. We're talking if my whole family left tomorrow, the population would be cut in half."

"That's so cool." I loved my dad, but it could get quiet with just the two of us.

"Sometimes," Lily agreed. "Other times it's like that family Thanksgiving dinner when the annoying relatives won't leave – *ever*. But I like Great-Aunt Ro."

Lily ran in and delivered her flowers, then we parked our bikes, and walked along the pier. The faint aroma of grease tinged the salty air. The food stands were just opening their doors, getting ready for the early lunch crowd. I listened as Lily told me about the different games of chance: which had the best prizes, which were the easiest to win, and which ones no one stood a chance at winning.

"Ready for a scare?" David called from his post at the haunted house.

The large Victorian manor was painted a dark purple with black trim. In the late morning light, the chipped and peeling paint was visible. Seagulls swooped overhead.

"You can't scare me," Lily boasted.

"That's what you think." David gestured towards Midnight Manor. "I bet you'll scream."

"You're on!" Lily grinned, delighted by the challenge. "Let's show him, Sara. Nothing can scare us!"

"Uh . . . well . . . I'm not really into haunted houses," I muttered. "I'll just hang here. You go."

"There's nothing scary in there, believe me," Lily prodded.

"I don't have any money for tickets—" I began.

"We don't need money. David'll let us in."

David nodded. "Just don't tell."

Lily linked her arm with mine. "Come on, Sara. You can't live in Stellamar and not laugh at Midnight Manor. It's, like, a requirement."

A woman had died in this house. Was she still in there – waiting for me? I didn't want to find out. I glanced at Lily's hopeful face. I really did want to be friends with her. I wanted to have fun and laugh at the Midnight Manor like generations of kids in Stellamar did.

"Let's do it," I agreed. I gazed at Midnight Manor. How scary could a run-down boardwalk attraction be – especially during the day?

A few minutes later, I was plunged into darkness. The sun, the boardwalk, the beach seemed miles away. Icy air swirled about me as I followed Lily through narrow hallways, sporadically lit by flickering electric candles. Doors on squeaky hinges swung open by themselves.

Lily giggled next to me. "Do you love it?"

"It's great." I gulped and kept close to her shadowy figure.

A low, painful moan echoed around us. Sticky spider webs brushed against my skin. I shivered. I really didn't want to be here.

Through a dark curtain, a zombie leaped out, making us shriek. Decomposed skin hung in pieces from its obviously fake head. I giggled nervously. Then I heard whispering. Again. Whispering behind me. I swivelled about. Other visitors? I peered into the darkness.

Nothing.

We walked on. More whispers. Closer now. Warm breath draped my neck. I spun around. Through the darkness, a face appeared. A skull with deep, empty eye sockets. Bony fingers touched me. I shrunk in fear . . . until Lily reached over and grabbed the skeleton's hands.

"Look, Sara!" she called. "We're doing the monster mash." She pretended to waltz with the fake skeleton. I realised that Lily knew I was scared and she was trying to distract me.

I laughed. I was annoyed at myself for being so timid, but grateful to Lily for being so cool about it.

She let go of the skeleton's hand and grabbed mine. "Onward!"

We ascended a dramatic curved staircase in the dim light. Fabric-draped walls reached up to an impossibly high ceiling. Portraits of men in Victorian-style clothing hung on the walls, their eyes tracking our every step. Mournful music played on a faraway organ. My eyes strained to glimpse the second-floor landing. Something was up there.

Something that glimmered and moved.

A woman in a long, pale dress.

The lights began to flicker.

I slowed my steps. Was it a spirit? The woman who died here?

She floated down the stairs. Towards me.

"Watch out, Sara!" Lily suddenly shrieked. She yanked my arm so hard, I fell to my knees – just in time to see the huge brass chandelier above me crash down! I screamed and covered my head. There was no time to move.

Lily doubled over in laughter. I peeked through my hands. The chandelier hung several feet over our heads, suspended by a thick cable. Then the cable magically pulled the chandelier back into place. An amazing special effect.

"I knew that would scare you!" Lily cried. "It's my favourite part. So cool, right?"

I grinned and finally relaxed. It was all a joke. Nothing in here was real. Even the woman on the stairs was just bedsheets and pulleys – not a spirit.

When we emerged in the blinding sunlight after more silly scares, Lily and I were laughing so hard I thought I'd have to find a bathroom.

Lily walked like a zombie towards David. "I repeat – so not scary. But Sara totally fell for the dropping chandelier. You gotta tell him, Sara, how you ducked for cover. Totally awesome."

But I couldn't speak.

There was someone leaving the haunted house.

Someone I recognised.

The old man with the cane floated out the side door, swirling around an oblivious group of people leaving the haunted house. They didn't see him, but I did. Because he was dead.

I began to shiver despite the sun beating down. My eyes remained glued to him.

"Hey, Sara," Lily coaxed.

He moved towards me. Then he opened his mouth and let out an anguished wail: *Sara!*

CHAPTER 7

He knows my name!

Every muscle in my body tensed. The blood stopped flowing through my veins. I was numb with fear.

He shimmered a few feet in front of me, yet he seemed to be everywhere.

Sara, Sara . . . The sound was more a rumble than a voice. And my name sounded like a moan.

He needed me.

Sara, Sa–ra!

He reached for me, groping the air. The numbness fell away. Dizziness invaded my body. My legs shook, and I feared I would fall.

"Hey, what's wrong? You don't look good." Lily was by my side.

I didn't trust myself to speak. My eyes remained locked on the old man's shimmery image.

"Sara, seriously. Are you sick?" Lily grabbed my arm.

The image faded, then was gone. As if he'd never really been there.

"I don't feel so good," I croaked. It was true. I felt as if I'd vomit.

"Do you want me to get you some water?" David asked.

I shook my head. "I'm going to go home."

"I'll go with you," Lily said.

I saw him again. Further down the pier. Waiting. Waiting for me.

"No," I replied. He quivered in the sun's glare.

"Of course I'm coming with you," Lily insisted. She began to lead me down the pier. Towards him.

I shook her off. "No!" I hadn't meant to sound so harsh.

Lily backed away, surprised.

"I'm sorry," I mumbled. "I've got to go, okay? I'm sorry—"

I started to run. My flip-flops slapped the planks as I picked up speed. I raced past him.

"Sara!"

I flung myself onto my bike, pedalling furiously. I was on Beach Drive before I realised it was Lily calling my name, not the spirit.

I'd messed it all up. Lily must have thought I was so rude.

My heart sunk as I turned towards home. It'd been a mistake to think I could have a best friend. Some kids were blissfully unaware that they were different. But I knew. I was different because I could see things others couldn't. And I was old enough to know that with most kids, different equalled weird. At least it had in California. I guessed it did in New Jersey, too.

I wished I could turn back and explain to Lily what I'd seen.

More than anything, I wished I could just be normal.

"See this thing?" My dad held up the tool. "It's called a hammer."

"I know what it's called."

"Oh, well, since you said you were helping, I thought you might be confused. You see, your camera doesn't actually repair anything." My dad's blue eyes danced as he teased me.

I squatted on the stair, focusing the lens on the pattern of the banister. The spokes looked like soldiers lined up at attention. "I'm documenting how you transform this house. Like one of those reality shows."

"And that's helping how?" he asked. He banged a nail to secure a wobbly spoke.

"In a very special way." I grinned at him, then snapped a close-up of the nail.

We worked side by side – him hammering, me photographing.

"You sure you don't want to play outside?" he asked for the tenth time that afternoon. "Maybe find that girl from down the street?"

I shook my head. I'd been in the house for the past two days. Unpacking. Helping Dad fix stuff. Avoiding the boardwalk. Avoiding Lily.

I felt bad about that. Not the boardwalk. I was never going near that haunted house again. But about Lily. She'd been texting me like crazy. I told her I was fine, but I'd pretended that I wasn't feeling well enough to go out.

I stopped taking pictures and leaned back on my

heels, listening. The floorboards above me creaked. Long then short.

They'd been creaking nonstop for days. It was the woman in the rocking chair in the pink bedroom. Trying to rock away her sadness. Every now and again her sobs echoed throughout the house. I insisted her door – actually *all* doors – stay closed.

"Dad," I began tentatively. "What about if we go back?"

"Go back where?" He brushed a splintered post with sandpaper.

"Home. To California."

He stopped sanding to focus on me. "This is our home, kiddo. Our new home."

"I don't like it. I don't like this town or this house." I hated how my voice came out like a whine.

His broad shoulders sagged. "Sara, it's always hard in the beginning. You just need to give it all a chance—"

"I did. It feels bad here," I said, my throat tight with emotion. "The boardwalk is . . . the haunted house . . . it's really haunted."

Dad looked visibly relieved. "Oh, kiddo, that's just your imagination. That's what they want you to think.

A haunted house is supposed to scare you—"

"It's more than that. There's this unhappiness here. This horrible, um, vibe—"

He dropped the sandpaper and reached for my hand. "Remember what we've talked about. You can't let your emotions overwhelm you." He gave my hand a reassuring squeeze. "A new place is always scary when you're by yourself. But school will start in a few weeks. You won't be so alone. You'll see more people and then—"

See more people? I wanted to scream. *Do you know how many people I can see? I see more people than anyone else in this town!*

But I didn't scream. I didn't say anything. I hated how worried my dad looked. I didn't want to make him look like that. I knew he was scared that I was too anxious – about everything. And I knew he blamed himself. I'd overheard him once on the phone with Aunt Charlotte. He felt he was messing up raising me alone.

"You're probably right," I agreed softly.

His face brightened. "That's my girl." He handed me a piece of sandpaper. Problem solved.

I smoothed the imperfections on the wood. Making it all look the same. After a while I spoke. "Why here? Why did you choose here?"

"Your mother and I always liked it. We lived in New Jersey when we were first married. Not too far from here. A few towns down the motorway." His lips turned up in a grin. Happy memories.

"Why didn't I know that?" I'd thought my dad had shared every story about my mum with me.

"It was only for a year. One year." He paused, as if transported back in time. "She loved the beach but hated the ocean. She'd walk for hours on the sand but wouldn't even put her feet in the water."

I savoured this nugget of information. So many of my dad's stories were about events but never about her. Who she was. What she thought and dreamed. "Why didn't she like the water?"

He shrugged. "She used to say that people should respect the power of nature. She believed that the ocean was way more powerful than she was, and so she knew not to tangle with it." He smiled. "Sometimes, she was silly like that."

"I don't think that's silly," I said. There *were* things

out there way more powerful than we were. Things I couldn't begin to understand.

That night I sat cross-legged on my bed, holding a framed photograph of my mother in my hands. I'd stared at this photo so often, I felt as if I knew her face better than my own. The same small nose as mine, the same dimples. Mum's face was longer and narrower than mine. And her cheekbones really stood out when she smiled, and mine don't do that. I traced the waves of her light blonde hair with my fingertips. It was the same pale blonde colour as mine. She sat on a large rock, her knees pulled up into her chest. She was smiling brightly at the camera. I knew my dad had taken the picture, and it made me happy to think she looked at him like that. I wished she were here. I wished I knew her.

"It's weird here, Mum," I said softly. My eyes sought hers.

The rocking chair down the hall creaked back and forth. The man with the sailor cap rapped on his bedroom window, as if trying to attract attention. Dad said houses make noises. That they "settle." I sighed. This house wasn't settling. Dead people were making the noise.

Then I asked her the question that had been on my mind for days: "Why are they here and you're not?"

These people were dead. My mum was dead. *If I could see them, could I see her?*

I closed my eyes and began to sway like I'd seen Lady Azura do. I hummed and tried to think of nothing but my mother. In my mind, I called for her.

If Lady Azura can summon a spirit, so can I.

I twirled my braided silver ring. It had belonged to my mother. It connected us. I called her name over and over. *Mum.*

I waited for the bed to shake. For something to happen. For a sign.

After a while, I opened my eyes.

The room was empty.

"Where are you?" I asked the photo. "I don't want all these other people. I want *you.*" Tears tickled the back of my eyes. It was so unfair. "Are you with them? Do you know what they want?"

There was no answer. Only the muffled sobs of the rocking-chair woman filtering through the walls.

I held up the photo, so we were nose-to-nose.

"Please help me understand," I whispered. "Please."

CHAPTER 8

My hand grazed the purple curtain before pushing it aside.

"There you are, child. Didn't you hear me calling?"

I'd been out back, trying to place my flip-flops casually on the grass, as if they'd been carelessly kicked off, so I could take a photo.

"Sorry," I replied. I stared in amazement. She stood by the back shelves of the fortune-telling room with a sparkling bright-blue stone in one hand and a soft, yellow cloth in the other. Rows and rows of colourful stones glimmered from the display.

"Don't be shy. Come closer." She beckoned to me. "I don't want to raise my voice in this room. The aura in here is delicately balanced. Can you feel it?"

I stood still and felt a floating feeling. That sense

that comes the instant before you open your eyes in the morning when you already know it's sunny and there's no school. "Yes," I said, my voice showing my surprise.

"Good. It's good you can feel it." She rubbed a whitish-green stone, bringing out its shine.

"These rocks are so pretty," I said.

"These are not rocks," she corrected. "Rocks are outside in the dirt. These are gemstones and crystals. They have powers."

"Powers?" I edged closer to the shelves. "What kinds?"

"Many different kinds. Light reflects off the gems and crystals, allowing their special energy to be absorbed into your body." She reached for a pale pink jagged crystal. "This is rose quartz. It helps you to forgive. The crystal next to it provides safe journey."

"What about this yellow one?" I pointed to a smooth, small stone.

"Citrine helps solve money problems," she explained. I briefly thought back to my dad and wondered if he did have money problems, could they be cured by a gemstone?

"Pink opal improves luck. Tiger's eye, jade and agate offer protection," Lady Azura continued.

"Protection from what?" I asked.

"Bad feelings, negative desires, evil." She pointed to a brown stone and a grey stone. "Pink tourmaline and smoky quartz are the most powerful against evil forces."

I reached for the quartz, but she blocked my reach. "It is not for you to choose," she cautioned. "The stone must choose you."

Choose me? I was back to not understanding her.

"I need you to fetch me something important," Lady Azura said.

"Okay." My gaze lingered on the two stones. Shields against evil. Would they work?

"Fresh fudge. Vanilla, to be exact. From Veda's Fudge Shop on the boardwalk," Lady Azura instructed.

"On the boardwalk?" I repeated. I knew where the fudge shop was. Across from the haunted house.

"Yes." She inhaled. "I can sense they are making a batch now. Veda's is like no others. I can taste the difference."

"But—" I couldn't go back there.

"Hurry, child. People are lining up. I can *feel* it." She motioned towards the curtain.

I didn't move.

Lady Azura paused, then grabbed both my hands with hers. She gazed intently at me. "Sara." Her bony fingers gripped so hard that blood pulsed in my veins. "You must face your fears."

"What?" I cried, startled.

"You cannot live in fear."

Does she know about the spirit at the haunted house? I wondered. Of all people, she'd believe me. She'd know what to do.

She flipped my hands over so my palms faced up. She traced the lines and grinned. "But good things are on your horizon. Very good. You shall soon meet a tall, dark stranger."

I tried to keep a straight face. She had to be kidding me. A tall, dark stranger? That was the lamest fortune-telling line ever. I was beginning to think Lily's mum was wrong. Lady Azura didn't speak the truth. She just made stuff up. I couldn't believe I'd come so close to telling her everything.

I walked to Beach Drive. Slowly. I figured there had to be a sweet shop in the town. I mean, it's a beach town.

Beach towns are drowning in fudge.

I was wrong. Lots of ice cream. Even saltwater taffy. But every store told me Veda's on the boardwalk was the only place for fudge. Figures.

Hey kiddo all good?

I glanced at my mobile phone. Dad was texting. Ever since I mentioned being unhappy a few days ago, he'd been checking in nonstop. He felt bad this job took up so much time, especially when school hadn't started yet.

Lady A wants fudge. I answered.

U like fudge. Buy some 2. Use the $ I gave U.

I sighed. He didn't get it. **Fudge store is by haunted house.**

U can do it. Remember mind over matter.

I wasn't so sure. Spirits weren't something I could just turn on and off like a light switch. I had no control.

U there kiddo? I can leave work in an hour and go w/ u if u want.

I bit my lip, gnawing the chapped skin. Even as nervous as I was, making him leave his office and drive thirty minutes so he could help me buy fudge seemed ridiculous.

No im good. I can do it. thx.

I made a plan. I would avoid the haunted house by walking along the opposite side of the pier. I'd keep my back turned and look only at the shops and rides on that side. I'd never have to see the haunted house. And no one would see me.

Lily had texted me that morning. She was helping some aunt or cousin who ran a hotel down the beach. I was glad. Everyone knew and noticed Lily on the boardwalk.

The line for fudge was out the door. As I waited my turn, I wondered again about Lady Azura. I tried to decide if she really had psychic powers. Her hokey fortune-telling and tea-leaf reading pointed to no. She couldn't see or hear Ronald. But, I reasoned, she did *conjure* Ronald's spirit and seemed to sense some stuff about me. Plus, she knew there'd be fresh fudge and a line. The evidence was pretty even for both sides.

"Have you ever tasted the fudge?" asked the woman in front of me. She'd come right off the beach. A mesh tunic barely covered her black bikini.

"No. Is it good?" I asked as we inched into the

shop. A blast of air-conditioning and concentrated sugar welcomed us.

"The best. So good I dream about it. Literally." She smacked her lips in anticipation. "On Tuesdays they always make the fresh vanilla fudge. Every vanilla fudge fanatic knows Tuesdays at two."

Lady Azura totally scammed me, I thought. *The whole town knows there's vanilla fudge for sale today.* I felt deflated. I realised that I was hoping Lady Azura would be for real. That I secretly wished she was kind of like me.

A perky teenage girl behind the counter finally cut my hunk of fudge and placed it in a white box. I moved down the line towards the register. I wondered when Lily would be back home. Pulling out my phone to text her, I felt the first pinpricks.

On my legs.

Like insects creeping up my skin, the sensation quickly covered my whole body. The store suddenly seemed extremely crowded. There wasn't enough air for all these people. I tried to inhale but couldn't fill my lungs. My fingers trembled as I squeezed the cardboard box.

He'd found me.

The old man with the cane stood beside me. He leaned heavily on the horse's head carved into the handle of his cane.

Please, he called. His body trembled.

I tried to look away. But turning my head made the room dip and my stomach heave. The sweet counter rippled and the floor swayed. Beads of sweat dotted my hairline. No one else saw him.

Please. Please help. His voice was thin. He pushed each word out with great force, as if digging deep for strength.

Disaster looms.

I wanted to run, but my body couldn't move. The desperation of his words wrapped around me.

Disaster is coming . . . time is running out.

I squeezed my eyes shut. Willing him and his words away.

Midnight Manor . . . His limbs shook with fear. A fear so extreme that I, too, began to shake.

His fear. My fear. There was no difference.

The walls pressed in. My knees gave way, and I slumped to the floor.

CHAPTER 9

"Oh, my gosh!" The woman in the black bikini squatted down beside me. I stared at her burgundy-polished toenails in a daze.

"Is she okay?" The salesgirl appeared at our side, her perkiness replaced by a worried frown. "Should I call an ambulance or something?"

"No, no!" I blurted. My face flushed as I sensed everyone's eyes upon me. "I'm fine." The heavy, squeezing feeling was gone.

I gazed around the store. *He* was gone.

My legs shook just the tiniest bit as I stood.

"Are you dehydrated?" the salesgirl asked. She was only a few years older than I was. "It's really hot out."

"I guess that's it," I agreed tentatively, still clutching the crushed box of vanilla fudge.

She brought me a glass of cool water and led me outside to a bench in the shade. She sat beside me as I drank. I liked that she didn't ask any more questions. She seemed to be happy to be taking a break. I had a weird feeling she was related to Lily too. I decided I definitely liked their huge family.

I sipped the water and allowed myself to peek across towards the haunted house. David stood at the ticket stand before a line of about ten people. He glanced up and gave me a curious stare. I pretended I didn't see him.

What I did see – at least in my mind – was the image of the old man. I tried to think of something else, to erase him completely. But I couldn't help myself.

What was he saying? What disaster?

I glanced again at Midnight Manor, the eerie music harmonising with the shrieks of a woman winning the ring toss and a man offering caramel corn. There didn't seem to be anything wrong.

I didn't know why he was bothering me or what he thought I could do. I shook my head. Only a few minutes ago that man . . . spirit . . . whatever . . . made me feel so horrible I collapsed. I wanted nothing to do with him. Ever.

I certainly wasn't going to help him.

"Ta-da!" Dad swung open the door to the larger room on the third floor.

"No way!" I ran inside, bouncing with excitement. "This is perfect!" I flung my arms around him, inhaling his familiar woodsy smell.

"I hope I set it up correctly." Dad beamed at me, clearly happy that I was happy.

How could I not be? He'd transformed the dusty room just for me. My computer rested on a white desk with a new photo printer. A huge wooden table, painted a sunny yellow, sat in the circular part of the room. All my crafting scissors and stencils, plus boxes of stickers, markers and coloured paper were arranged on the table. He'd painted one wall the same bright yellow and glimpses of the blue-grey water of the bay were visible through the many windows.

"Oh, it's so amazing! Thank you." I hurried over to the desk. "I can't believe you got me a photo printer."

Dad came up behind me. "I knew you wanted one.

Maybe it will help you pass the rest of the summer—"

"It totally will!" I bent over its shiny black surface. "Can I see how it works? Is it wireless?"

"Of course." Dad busied himself with unwinding cords. He loved this kind of stuff – putting things together, fixing things that were broken. "I had this old house hooked up to the Internet while you were out exploring on your bike the other day. Not easy, believe me." He pulled out the printer's cord and knelt below the desk. "Hmmmm . . . that's the curse of an old house."

"Curse?" I asked.

"This enormous room has only one outlet. And if you plug in your computer, printer and the two lamps, you'll overload the circuit. An overload could burn the whole house down." He lifted himself up. "That's what happens when the future tries to interact with the past."

"So the printer won't work up here?"

"I can fix it. In a perfect world, I'd rewire the entire house. Actually, maybe I could. I read an article once. . ." He was still talking as he headed towards the stairs. "Let me see if I can rustle up a power strip in the meantime."

I knew he'd make it all work. He always did. I sat on the stool by the large table and grabbed a piece of paper and a marker. I began to sketch an idea for a new photo collage.

Except for trips to Elber's for Lady Azura, I made up my mind to spend the last days of summer up here in my happy, yellow hideaway. Far from the haunted house.

But a few days later, I was back inside Midnight Manor.

I wished I hadn't agreed to go inside. Without Lily, the house seemed much darker, much scarier. The flickering electric candles cast eerie shadows on the walls.

I followed the winding hallways in a daze. My eyes darted about nervously, waiting for the fake zombie or fake skeleton to pop out. Nothing. No scares. No fake moans or recorded shrieks.

Where was everything? Wasn't it working?

Suddenly, no scares felt scarier. I could hear my own breath. A heavy silence descended. I was alone. Alone in Midnight Manor.

I moved forwards, quickening my pace through a screen of cobwebs. The narrow hallway seemed to stretch on forever. Where was the exit? I wondered. Then I heard a *thump*.

Then another. *Thump, thump.*

In front of me. Somewhere in the darkness.

"Who's there?" I called.

Thump, thump. Footsteps. I wasn't alone.

"Hello?" My voice echoed back.

I rounded a corner, my heart pounding, and spotted two boys up ahead. One blond, one dark-haired. They both glanced back in my direction, then hurried into the shadows. I squinted. The dark-haired boy looked familiar. Was he Lily's brother? I wasn't sure.

"Joey!" I called. "Joey, wait up." I jogged forward.

The boys disappeared around another corner.

I ran faster. My breath came out in ragged pants. The hallway opened into a large room. Mirrors covered every wall. I exhaled loudly. The Room of Mirrors. I'd been here with Lily.

I whirled around. Dozens of reflections of me stared out. I was on every wall. Even the ceiling. Me, me, me.

I spotted the boys in the far corner of the room. Or was I seeing their reflections? I wasn't sure. There seemed to be dozens of boys.

"Hey, Joey, wait—" I began.

A chill tickled the back of my neck. There was a woman in the mirror. Her thin flesh was pulled tautly along the protruding bones of her face. White hair fanned out from her scalp. The colour in her irises had faded, leaving her eyeballs an eerie, deathly white.

There's only one of her, I thought. *She's not a reflection. She's trapped in the mirror!*

My eyes darted around the room, desperate for a way out. No doors. No windows. Just mirrors. Even the door I'd come in through had melted into glass.

I gulped in fear as her skeletal arms broke through the shiny surface. Her fingers circled Joey's neck and she began to squeeze. Tighter, tighter. Joey's eyes bulged as he struggled to free himself. Dozens of Joeys were reflected around the room, all writhing. Then the real Joey spotted me.

"Sara!" he choked. "Help me—"

The fingers tightened. His skin lost colour. His body grew limp.

I have to help. I reached out. The hands released him – and they grabbed for me.

CHAPTER 10

I couldn't stop screaming.

"Sara! Sara, you're okay."

My dad's voice. His hand on my shoulder. "A dream, kiddo. Just a dream."

I blinked. The mirrors were gone. The first light of dawn broke through the gap in my shades. My nightshirt stuck to my skin, clammy with sweat. I pushed myself onto one elbow and met my dad's worried gaze.

"You were screaming." He ran a hand through his bed-matted hair. "But whatever it was, it's not real, okay?"

I nodded, still too shaken to speak.

"What was it about?" he asked gently.

My mouth was extremely dry. A dull ache circled

my jaw, as if I'd been clenching my teeth. "The haunted house."

"Oh, Sara, you can't let that place upset you so much." He shook his head. "I hate that you still have nightmares. I wish I knew how to stop them."

I'd been having nightmares since I was about four years old. Dad thinks it's the usual monsters and witches and stuff. He doesn't know that the dreams started when *they* showed up.

"There was this horrible spirit," I started. "In the haunted house. She came at me through a mirror. And there's another spirit there. A man . . . with a cane—"

"Listen." He rubbed my back, the way he's done for so many years when I've woken frightened. "It's not right that a boardwalk haunted house is keeping you up at night. I have a solution. We'll go there together. This weekend. We'll conquer it together and make your fear go away."

I peeled a piece of blue nail polish from my thumbnail.

He didn't get it. Sure, we could go there together. But he'd never see what I see or hear what I hear. He'd never understand. They were never going away.

"What do you think, Sara?"

I looked up at my dad. I thought he looked tired. I thought he looked worried. "I think that might be okay."

"Get some rest." He pulled the duvet up over my shoulders and padded down the hallway to his room.

I switched on the lamp by my bed. There was no way I could go back to sleep. I lay there, listening to the floorboards creak under the rocking chair. The sad woman was awake too. I suddenly wondered why all the spirits I saw seemed unhappy. Was that why they were still around?

My thoughts kept circling back to the old man. I didn't want to think about him. He scared me a lot more than the rest of them. But why? Was it because he spoke to me? I didn't think that was it. Not totally, at least. I couldn't figure it out. I turned the question around in my mind until I landed upon an answer.

He was the only one who wanted something from me.

The damp sand chilled my toes as I bent down and scooped up a white half-moon shell. I tucked it among the growing collection of shells and sea glass nestled in the pouch pocket of my grey oversize sweatshirt. The weak rays of early morning sun glimmered on the water.

Dad and Lady Azura were still asleep. Most of Stellamar was still asleep. Only the fishing boats far out on the ocean and committed joggers on the sand were awake with me.

I knew Dad would be angry to find me gone. I left a note and had my phone on, but I knew I'd still hear about it. It wasn't like me to disobey rules. This morning, though, I just had to get out. Figure things out.

I inhaled the humid sea air. Thick grey clouds blanketed the sky. The foam-capped waves broke rapidly on the shore. Today wasn't going to be a beach day. I was fine with that. I'd found an old wooden tray in one of the rooms, and Lady Azura said I could have it. I planned to decoupage it with the photos of shells and sea life I'd taken, along with real shells and sea glass I'd collected. It'd be a 3-D collage that'd be useful, too. Maybe I'd send it to Aunt Charlotte.

A wiry woman with a long metal stick wandered

several feet ahead. She waved it along the sand, searching for buried treasure – loose change and rings that slipped off fingers. I was curious to see what she'd find.

Frantic splashing made my head turn. I gasped. A girl with dark hair bobbed in the choppy waves. Seagulls cried overhead as I craned my neck to see her. No one else was out swimming.

"Lily?" I jogged in her direction, the shells jangling with each quickened step. "Lily?" I was having trouble seeing her now.

What was Lily doing in the ocean?

Cold water lapped my ankles, tingling my feet, as I ran towards her. She seemed to shimmer in the sparkling water. "Lily!"

She didn't respond. Instead she faded in and out. There and then not there. Slowly, she dissolved into the air.

I kicked the sand angrily. She wasn't Lily. She wasn't even alive. A spirit forever swimming in the Atlantic. I hated the confusion. I hated not knowing who was real.

I continued down the beach. I kept my eyes on the sand, concentrating on shells and sea glass. When I finally looked up, the beach entrance to the boardwalk stood before me. I gazed up the wooden stairs.

I thought of my dad. He wanted me to stop being afraid. It was definitely faster to get home this way than going back down the beach. I didn't have to go anywhere near the haunted house, I reasoned. I should just do it. Right?

I hesitated, then began to climb.

The colour and energy were missing from the boardwalk on this overcast morning. All the stands and booths were boarded up. No laughter, no shrieks, no piped-in music. Just the cries of the seagulls and the footsteps of elderly power walkers.

"Storm's coming," a woman carrying a Yorkie in a pink jumper warned.

My hair blew across my face as the wind picked up. Flags along the pier flapped, and the sky grew darker. I glanced down the pier. The rides and games were closed. Midnight Manor loomed like a purple mountain against the grey clouds.

Every logical part of me knew I should turn right and head towards Beach Drive and home. I wanted to. I didn't want to make Dad worry. But my body wasn't communicating with my brain. My feet walked down the pier as if guided by a remote control. There wasn't a choice. There was only one direction to go.

I don't want to be here, I thought as a powerful force drew me ever closer to the haunted house.

No one was around. The attraction was closed. I stared up at the abandoned house. In the quiet, it seemed almost harmless. The MIDNIGHT MANOR sign squeaked on its hinges as gusts of wind rippled off the water. I leaned back on my heels, surveying the old house. No sadness came from the building. Everything seemed fine. Maybe I was overreacting. Maybe Dad was right.

I swallowed, then gagged as a sour taste invaded my throat. Chills snaked along my skin. A throbbing pulsed in my temple. I realised that I wasn't alone.

He was back.

I turned to run, but the old man blocked my path.

I need you . . . there is no more time. His strained voice reverberated in my ears. No longer could I hear the wind. I could hear only him.

I tried to dodge around him, but his frail form was everywhere. I couldn't escape.

Any day now . . . help save the children . . . stop . . . stop the tragedy . . . His voice pleaded.

"What tragedy?" I cried. "I don't understand. What tragedy?"

He didn't react. His eyes remained slightly unfocused. But the weight of his need pushed upon me, squeezing my lungs.

"Do you hear me?" I asked in a shrill voice I almost didn't recognise as my own.

But he didn't. This wasn't a conversation. I realised that I could hear him, but he couldn't hear me.

Save them . . . help them . . .

His desperation weighed on me. Spots appeared before my eyes, and my head ached. I had to get away.

"No!" I screamed. "I'm not helping you! Ever!"

I wrenched my body away as a huge gust of wind rolled in. The haunted house sign rocked violently on its rusted hinges. Then there was a sharp *snap!* The ancient wood splintered directly above my head.

I dodged, just as the sign crashed to the ground.

"Sara!" David ran towards me from the entrance to the pier, probably on his way to work.

I gazed in amazement at the broken sign strewn

near my feet. So close. It had almost hit me. I raised my eyes slowly to the old man. He shimmered by the fractured sign, pointing to it with his cane.

This is what happens. . . . He slid towards me, until he was just inches away. *It is up to you . . . without your help they will die. It is up to you.*

CHAPTER 11

"Oh, wow! I saw that." David ran up to me, panting.

"Huh?" My eyes roamed the pier. The old man had vanished.

I tried to focus on David's concerned face but kept hearing the man's words. *It is up to you.*

"Did any of the wood hit you on the head? You look out of it." David spoke fast. "Maybe I should go get someone."

"No, no, I'm fine. Really." I forced another smile. I was getting good at these forced smiles and pretending that everything was all right when it clearly wasn't. "It totally missed me."

"Say the alphabet backwards," he commanded.

"What?"

"I need you to say the alphabet backwards. To

make sure you don't have a head injury," he insisted. "They taught us that in Nature Guides."

"Seriously?" I sighed when he nodded. "Okay. Z, Y, X, W, V . . . uh . . . Listen, I don't know the alphabet backwards, but my head is fine. I didn't even get scraped." I spun so he could see I was unharmed.

"Well, you're lucky, then." He surveyed the mess in front of the haunted house. "I'm going to have to call the guy at Pier Management to clean up and get a new sign. He's not going to be happy."

I trailed David to the ticket stand. He pulled his mobile phone from his backpack and made the call about the sign.

I wondered about the sign. Did it crack because it was old and the winds from the coming storm destroyed it? Or did the spirit make it fall because I said I wouldn't help him? I pushed back the hair blowing in my eyes and stared at the splintered wood. The old man had definitely pointed to it. Was the broken sign a threat or was it some sort of clue?

"This place is a dump," David remarked when he finished.

"So . . . do you think it's unsafe?" I followed him through the swirling wind to the side door of the mansion.

He chuckled. "I knew you were scared."

"I'm not scared," I insisted. "Well, okay, maybe a little."

"All the monsters and ghouls are safe and sound." He unlocked the side door and flicked a switch, bathing the mansion in light.

"I wasn't worried about them," I quipped, stepping into the small utility room beside him. "I was worried about the real people. The people who almost get crushed by falling signs." I couldn't believe I'd just said that. I'd never been sarcastic before. Something about this town was making me bolder.

"Point taken." David opened a huge panel on the wall and ran down a row of switches with his fingers. "I assume this place is safe. It's just run-down. The company that owns it isn't interested in fixing it."

"Really? That seems so wrong."

He shrugged. "I complain all the time, but they

just ignore me. They think I'm some dumb teen."

"Which you're not."

"Which I'm not." He grinned. "I see Lily hasn't poisoned you yet. I need to do the morning run-through. I do the first check, then Mike, the manager, does the final one before we open. Do you want to see Midnight Manor unplugged? The acoustic version?" he asked.

"Sure." I knew I should be getting home, but suddenly I wanted to see exactly what was in this house.

"What's wrong? You have that weird worried look again."

"There's something about this place," I began. "It feels . . . off. Like something bad is going to happen. Do you ever feel it?"

"Yes."

"Really?" I couldn't control my excitement.

"Yes, I feel that people are going to think this haunted house stinks and stop coming, and I'm never going to get enough money for that camera." He pretended to shiver. "Bad feelings."

"Very funny," I muttered.

I followed David through the house as he checked each room.

Midnight Manor looked so normal with all the lights on and all the mechanical scares off. I pulled my camera from my back pocket and snapped photos of random objects – brass doorknobs, mechanical skeleton hands, old candelabras.

"Look how much stuff needs repair." David pointed out tracks to be oiled, dozens of lightbulbs to be changed, curtains to be seamed. I took photos of it all. I wasn't going to use this stuff for a collage. I was hoping that the old man's disaster would show itself through my lens. But nothing here looked as if it'd cause a tragedy.

"You know that bad feeling?" I decided to try one more time. "I just feel that something's going to happen here."

"Kind of like a sixth sense, huh?" David said. "Okay. What's going to happen?"

"I don't know," I admitted.

"Do you know *when* it's going to happen?"

I shook my head "No."

He laughed. "Your psychic powers need work.

You don't know too much, do you?"

I blushed. He was right. I was more confused than ever.

"Mermaid's tears." Lady Azura peered over my shoulder that afternoon on the front porch.

I gazed up from sorting the treasure from my morning beach walk. "What?"

She pointed to the sea glass I'd gathered. "That's what my friends and I called sea glass when I was young."

"Really? Why?" I sat cross-legged. Shells and glass surrounded me in carefully organised piles.

Lady Azura adjusted the enormous brim of her woven, oversized sun hat. It was something a glamorous 1940s movie star would have worn. I wasn't sure why she had it on, because the sky was still overcast and a light rain drummed the porch roof. It must go with the long white dress, I decided.

"The story starts with Poseidon, god of the sea," Lady Azura began. "One day, a sailor's boat was caught in the powerful winds and the waves of a storm. The sailor was being pulled under and would surely drown, and the mermaids swam to help. Poseidon, angered that the mermaids dared to interfere with his control of the sea, banished them to below the surface. They were never to help another human in peril. The mermaids were so sad, that whenever they saw humans swallowed by the sea, they'd cry and their tears would harden and wash up to shore."

I scooped the green and clear glass in my hand. The glass was no longer sharp and angular. Decades of being in the sea, pounded by waves against the rocks, had smoothed the glass and made it frosted. "That's a neat story." I reached up and placed a few glass pebbles in Lady Azura's hand.

She lifted her arched, penciled eyebrows in surprise. This was the closest I'd come to a gesture of friendship since I'd arrived. "When I was a child, back in the Dark Ages, there were so many more colours. Browns, blues, even reds. People no longer toss bottles in the sea, I suppose. Recycling and all that."

"That's a good thing," I reminded her. "Keeps the water clean."

"Yes." She took several steps backwards and

began to lower herself onto the hanging double swing.

I sucked in my breath. The spirit knitting the scarf that never grew was there. Lady Azura was about to sit on her lap! True, Lady Azura was tiny, but the spirit was old. My eyes grew wide.

The spirit continued to knit, never dropping a stitch. Lady Azura paused, then gracefully shifted to the right, bypassing the spirit's translucent lap and landing next to her instead. She grinned slyly at me.

I gazed between the living and dead women. Should I say something? I had no idea what. I turned back to sorting shells.

Lady Azura watched me silently for a while. "I am receiving an unhappy vibe from your aura." Her voice had taken on a husky, mystical quality.

"You hardly need to be psychic for that. I don't love it here. No offense." Except for meeting Lily, I wished we'd never moved to this spooky shore town.

Lady Azura breathed deeply several times. "I don't think Stellamar is the cause," she said quietly. Both her palms were pressed together and she seemed focused

SARANORMAL

on her wrinkled fingers. "It is not the present that brings you unhappiness. This feeling is old. Older than you." She sighed. "We have all felt it."

Slowly she separated her hands, revealing the sea glass pieces in her palm. "Some things are not clear. Some things look one way and then turn out to be something else." She pinched a pebble of pale green glass and held it up.

"I don't understand." My voice came out in a shaky whisper.

"Sara, we often don't get to choose our path. Sometimes, like with this piece of glass, we get pulled along by the current. We drift, unsure." She fixed her steady gaze on me. "But there is always a choice. The choice to float along or the choice to change direction and swim."

"Swim?" I repeated. Of course, I knew she didn't want me to actually swim, but what did she want me to do?

"Action, my child." She titled her face towards the sun. "I am advocating action. If you don't like something, change it."

There were a lot of things I didn't like.

I didn't like living here.

I didn't like seeing spirits.

I didn't like the old man's mysterious instructions.

I didn't like Lady Azura speaking in riddles.

After a moment's hesitation, I scooped the shells and sea glass into a bag and stood. I knew how to fix the last one.

"I'm ready for a change . . . of scenery," I announced with my own sly smile. "I'm going upstairs to work on this project." I waved, then strolled into the house.

When I glanced back, Lady Azura's scarlet lips were raised in an amused grin. I had a feeling that wasn't the action she was talking about.

A few minutes later, I stood at the bottom of the stairs, transfixed by the thick purple curtains to my right. Lady Azura's rooms. All week I'd been feeling a pull . . . a tug . . . guiding me in there. Suddenly, it seemed extremely urgent to enter.

I could hear Lady Azura's muffled voice from the porch. The mailman had sauntered up and leaned against the railing, visibly happy to get out of the rain and chat for a while.

Quietly, I stole across the foyer and slipped through the fabric. My heart pounded in my ears. I had never sneaked into anyone's private place before.

My eyes slowly adjusted to the dim light. The curtains were drawn. The cinnamon aroma surrounded me. My nerves tingled, suddenly alive. The air felt electric with promise. Anything seemed possible.

I brushed my fingers over the clear, smooth crystal ball and peered inside. Nothing. I held a vial of blue liquid to my nose. It smelled faintly of maple.

Then I spotted the gemstones.

I edged closer. My eyes danced over the colours and shapes. Lady Azura's husky laugh drifted in from outside.

My hand reached like a magnet seeking metal for the pink tourmaline. The gemstone she said kept evil away. The opaque, rosy stone warmed my palm. I squeezed my fingers around it and closed my eyes. My heartbeat slowed. Muscles in my neck relaxed. A feeling of strength spread throughout my limbs.

The mailman was saying good-bye. My eyes blinked open.

In a flash, I darted back through the curtain and

hurried up the stairs, the pink tourmaline still warm in my hand.

I sat on my bed and looked at the oval stone for a long time. *Protection from evil spirits.* I had no right to take it. I knew I should return it. Yet, I couldn't. Not now.

This stone will help me, I decided.

I traced a vein of grey snaking through the pink stone.

The old man desperately needed help. *My help.*

Maybe Lady Azura was right. Maybe it was time to dive in.

CHAPTER 12

"Again?" Lily wrinkled her nose. "Okay, spill it. Do you have a crush on David?"

I stopped mid-slurp, nearly choking on my frozen lemonade. "What?" I screeched. "No way!"

"Look, I'm just saying, this is the third day in a row that you've made us hang out by the haunted house." Lily's bangle bracelets clanged as she waved her hand. "I mean, don't take this wrong, it's kind of boring watching people trot in and out. And I know you're scared of going inside it. So, logic tells me we're there because of David." She gave a self-congratulatory grin, as if she'd discovered the answers to the test before the teacher handed it out.

"I'm so not crushing on David," I insisted as we headed once again down the pier towards Midnight Manor.

"Uh-huh, like I'm believing that." She raised her sunglasses and narrowed her eyes at me.

"I'm not into him. Just friends. Really." I knew Lily didn't believe me. But what could I say? *Hey, Lily, we've been staking out this haunted house waiting for some unknown person, who could be dead or alive, to make some disaster happen so I can try to save people I don't know.* She'd think I was loony.

An hour later, I was starting to wonder if maybe I was.

We sat on the bench outside Midnight Manor. Lily flipped through a teen magazine, deciding which Academy Awards dresses would look good on her. I watched the people by the entrance. Two little boys with squirt guns. A tired mum wiping candy floss from a wriggling toddler's chubby cheeks. A boy on a skateboard nearly running down a dad holding the hands of sand-crusted twins. The eerie melody boomed, and kids tumbled out the exit door high-fiving and laughing.

No one the least bit threatening.

Last night, Dad even came with me. We went through the house together. He was impressed that I got through without screaming. He didn't know that I'd been through the house many times now. I knew when every ghoul would jump and every chandelier would fall. But I didn't know what I was supposed to do.

I stood and walked over to David. About twenty people waited at the ticket stand. "Hey, how's it going?"

"The same as it was going a half hour ago when you last asked." He ripped a ticket then gave me a wary look. "What's up with you?"

"Nothing." I tried to look casual. "So . . . see anyone suspicious coming through?"

"Suspicious how?"

"I don't know. Mean-looking. Like someone plotting something." I surveyed the line. Normal folks toting beach bags and kids.

"Hey," I said, suddenly panicked. "Do you search bags? Do you check that they're not carrying weapons or dangerous stuff?"

"Seriously?" David looked amused. "You've got to lay off the TV, Sara. This is a boardwalk at the beach. We've got no bad guys here, no terrorists. The only crimes are ugly bathing suits and littering."

"You never know . . ." I took a closer look at David. What did I know about him? Sure, he was Lily's cousin and seemed like a good guy, but maybe he was going to cause the disaster. It was always the one who looked innocent. Maybe he—

"Sara!" Lily shook me out of my sinister thoughts. "My mum just texted. She wants me to get something from Great-Aunt Ro. You coming?"

"Sure." I glanced back at Midnight Manor as I followed her through the wall of sunscreen-slicked bodies. Lily snaked through with practised skill. I bobbed and weaved a few steps behind, glad her magenta top was easy to keep in sight. Voices called out greetings. Uncles, aunts, cousins. Eyes watched us and watched out for us every step we took.

"In here, Sara!" Lily entered a small, circular building at the far end of the boardwalk. I pushed open the glass door to find a short, squat woman with cropped curls crushing Lily to her expansive chest. "An angel. This one is an angel." She pulled Lily back a few inches and flicked her chin with her thumb. "An angel with a mischievous streak, no?"

"Who, me?" Lily widened her eyes as if in an anime comic.

"Yes, you." Great-Aunt Ro turned to me. "This one overflows with brio, no?" She noticed my blank look. "Brio. Energy. Liveliness. No?"

I smiled. "Definitely."

"So Aunt Ro, Mum says you have an envelope you need me to run to cousin Bobby?" Lily hoisted herself onto the low information desk beside the pamphlets on charter boat rides and mini golf and started chatting with Ro. We were the only ones in the building.

I felt awkward just standing there. There was nothing to look at in the small room except framed photographs of people's heads spaced evenly along the taupe walls. The only sound, besides Lily's excited chatter, was the hum of the air conditioner. I studied a photo of a famous fisherman, a famous real estate guy, and a famous restaurant owner. They were all boring.

". . . and then Christy told my mum that Lorette wasn't going to the bridal shower. . ." I tuned Lily and her aunt out and continued the mind-numbing tour of Stellamar's celebrities.

Goosebumps suddenly rose from my skin. Was it the air-conditioning or something else? I slid my hand into my shorts pocket and touched the pink stone as I turned toward the other side of the room. I sucked in my breath.

The old man stared straight at me.

I stared back at him in amazement. This time I could see his face clearly. His thick brows, the furrow of his forehead, the crinkles around his eyes. I wrapped my fingers around the gemstone. *Protection from evil,* I chanted as I edged closer and examined his photograph on the wall.

A small gold nameplate read: GEORGE MARASCO.

The spirit had a name.

This was the first time I'd ever known one of their names. A shiver rolled down my spine as I ran my finger over the letters. George was real. Or, he'd once been real.

"Who is he?" I asked. My back was to Lily and her aunt. I couldn't stop staring at the photo.

Aunt Ro waddled over. She peered up at the name. "Marasco. Hmmm. I can't say that I know. Silly of me, since I sit here with these guys ogling me all day." She headed back to the desk and began pecking at the computer's keys. "Seems George Marasco was a big deal around here a long time ago. It says he developed the pier back in 1925. It was his idea to move the haunted house from the bluffs and turn it into Midnight Manor."

I stiffened. It made sense that the old man was connected with the house.

"Hmmm . . . George was a pretty nifty guy," Ro continued. "He used his own money to keep the boardwalk going during the Great Depression. For the next three decades, he was a real fixture on the pier, greeting guests and even letting families who couldn't pay enjoy the rides for free."

"That's nice. They never let you on the rides now without paying," Lily remarked.

"Everyone liked this guy. In fact, his nickname was Grandpa George because he – oh, wait, I definitely remember him now." Ro's eyes brightened. "He was quite old when I was a kid—"

"Why was he called that?" I interrupted.

"The kids came up with it because he was so nice. Always gave us sweets and told us riddles." She scrolled down the Web page. "Wow, this brings me back. Look at these pictures of the pier and the haunted house from the fifties."

Lily and I crowded around the screen. Lily let out a low whistle.

Midnight Manor sparkled with fresh paint, no traces of the years of wear caused by ocean winds and salt. The people enjoying ice-cream cones and pizza slices looked as if they'd stepped out of an old-fashioned movie.

"A big corporation bought the pier about ten years ago. Some guy in some office somewhere runs it all and that's why it's neglected. It's missing the human touch," Aunt Ro muttered.

"What happened to Grandpa George?" I asked.

"He died."

I nodded. I knew that. "How?" I prodded.

Aunt Ro squinted at the screen. "Car accident in 1967. Oh, that's sad. He was on his way to speak at a benefit for disadvantaged children."

I thought about George Marasco for a long time that afternoon. The old man with the cane had been a good guy in life. I didn't think that changed once you died. I mean, niceness didn't just go away. It couldn't.

I wished that knowing who he was would help me understand what he needed me for. But I couldn't figure it out. What was going to happen?

After a while, Lily had to go home. I told her I was going to stay longer, just hang out.

Lily smirked. "David gets off at five today, I think."

"That's not why I'm staying. Come on. I told you I'm not into him."

"Like I'm convinced." She wiggled her eyebrows knowingly.

I returned to my bench and watched the haunted house. An hour passed. Then another.

The air around me grew thick. A slight tingling erupted in my foot and crept up my leg.

I was not watching alone.

Grandpa George hovered beside me. Silent.

Waiting, too, for something to happen.

This time I did not run away.

CHAPTER 13

"Twenty-four. Lucky number twenty-four!" cried the guy behind the stand.

Dad rechecked the ticket he held in his hand. He frowned.

"Not twenty-four?" I guessed.

"Sixteen." He pulled out another dollar from his wallet.

"You don't have to," I said. "I know I said the green frog is cute and all, but I took lots of photos of him. I don't need to take him home."

Dad looked wistfully at the line of stuffed frogs behind the roulette wheel. He'd tried eight times already. "Next one's going to be lucky," he promised.

I laughed. "One more, then we're going for food. I'm getting hungry."

Dad chose number three. He was having a

good time. He'd taken off work and we'd spent the day together, fixing up Lady Azura's house in the morning and playing the boardwalk games in the afternoon. So far he'd won me a stuffed baseball bat with eyes and a fuzzy pig puppet. Every few minutes, I found myself glancing towards Midnight Manor. Everything always looked the same. For days it'd looked the same.

I wished I could shake the horrible feeling of impending doom. *Disaster looms.* It was all I thought about. I couldn't concentrate – even on the fun things, like winning a stuffed frog.

"Dad," I began, as we walked away from the spinning wheel empty-handed. I had to tell someone. "This strange thing happened at the haunted—"

"Hey, Sara, what'd you win?" Lily bounded over, her long, wet hair fanning behind her. She wore cotton shorts over a damp indigo tankini.

I held up the two stuffed toys.

"Ooh, she's like Miss Piggy's less glamorous cousin." Lily popped the pig puppet on her hand. "Hello, Mr Collins," she squeaked in what I assumed was her talking pig voice.

"Hello to you, too, Lily and—" Dad paused and glanced over my shoulder.

"Miranda. That's my friend, Miranda," Lily supplied in her normal voice.

I snuck a look at the tall girl with honey-coloured hair beside Lily. Her eyes were hidden behind dark sunglasses. She gave the slightest nod hello.

"We just came from the beach. We're getting ice cream. Do you want to come, Sara?" Lily bounced on her toes. I'd noticed before that she rarely stayed still.

I hesitated. I'd actually started to tell dad about George – and maybe even *all* the dead people. But now I didn't think I'd be able to explain it. Not here. Not now. I eyed Miranda. Would she think I was barging in?

"Yes, go with them," Dad encouraged. "You said you were hungry." He pulled out his wallet and handed me a twenty. "I'm heading home – maybe work on that back patio. Just be back in an hour. Have fun, okay, kiddo? And stay together." He grinned at me, then at Lily and Miranda. Clearly pleased I'd made friends.

Clearly pleased I was normal.

I walked with Lily and Miranda. Lily did most of the talking. She tried to include me but it was hard.

The two of them had been in the same class at school and the same dance class for years.

"I'm signing up for contemporary and jazz," Miranda announced. She turned to me. "What about you?"

"I don't dance," I said. My eyes drifted down to my white flip-flops. Whenever I felt unsure, I studied my shoes. I was becoming quite the footwear expert.

"Really?" Miranda wrinkled her nose, as if I'd announced I hated chocolate.

"Uh-uh."

"Sara's always taking pictures," Lily said. "She's really good at it, aren't you, Sara?"

I shrugged. "Maybe—"

"Ohhh, take our picture!" Miranda cried when she noticed the digital camera in my hand.

"People photography really isn't my thing," I mumbled.

"Why not?" Miranda demanded.

"Please. Just a few," Lily begged, saving me from an explanation.

"Okay." I scanned the pier. The crowds had thinned already. The rides closed early on Mondays. My eyes landed on the bench in front of Midnight Manor. My bench. At least that's how I thought of it now. "How about there?" I suggested.

Miranda stood on the bench. She threw her head back and placed a hand on her hip. "Come on, Lily, let's pose."

Lily scrambled up beside her. As they arranged themselves, I peered through the camera screen at David.

He looked at his mobile phone, then at the group of kids waiting before him. The kids pleaded with him. He consulted his phone again.

"Hey, Sara, I can't strike this pose forever," Lily called.

I turned back and snapped a few photos.

"I really shouldn't let you guys in, you know. I mean the rides are closing, and I could lose my job. . ." David's voice drifted towards me.

"Let's get ice cream. I'm thinking cookies n' cream or mint chip," Lily said.

"Okay, okay, fine. Stop begging. You guys can be the last ones in." I watched David take the six kids' tickets and usher them through the front door.

The evening light suddenly faded, as if a huge shade had been snapped shut. The night grew dark. And cold.

"Hey, Sara, you listening? What flavour is your fave?" Lily's voice floated in from somewhere in the distance.

I couldn't turn away from the haunted house's door. I shivered. Something felt wrong. Very wrong.

"Sara," Lily tried again. "Don't you want to come?"

I frantically searched the front of the house. What was wrong? What was happening? Nothing seemed out of the ordinary. David hung a CLOSED sign. People wandered past. But I could feel it. Darkness.

"I don't want to stand here all night," Miranda complained.

"Sara—" Lily tugged the hem of my shirt.

"Oh, um . . ." I saw Miranda waiting impatiently several feet away. "I'll catch up with you in a second," I told Lily.

"You sure?" Lily seemed conflicted.

"Sure. Be right there." I forced the fake smile again.

Tentatively I stepped towards the house. Chills caused my body to tremble. My eyes canvassed every inch of the exterior. Why did it all look fine? Every nerve in my body told me it wasn't fine.

"What's up with you?" David asked when I stood before him.

"You know that bad feeling I told you about?" I couldn't look at him. The house. I had to watch the house.

"I guess."

He didn't remember, I could tell. "Could you check everything out now? Please?"

"I'm checking for what again?"

"I don't know. But disaster is on its way—"

David let out a deep laugh. "I never pegged you for one of those wacky doomsday people."

I hated that he laughed. The iciness in the air grew colder. I shivered.

"Sara," Lily called.

I glanced over at her. Then at the house.

"Oh, all right." David waved his arm dismissively. "I'll look around for your Great Evil. Go eat ice cream 'cause you're starting to freak me out."

"Really?"

"Really."

"Hey, listen." Lily returned to my side. "You shouldn't be worried about Miranda. She likes you. She's supernice if you get to know her, it's just at first she's a bit harsh. So you should come with us—"

Lily's soft brown eyes brimmed with genuine

warmth. She was trying really hard to include me. To be my friend. And I was acting, well, weird.

I *so* didn't want to be the weird girl here.

This house isn't my problem, I decided abruptly. I couldn't let it ruin my new life. I took a deep breath. "I'm thinking raspberry chip. I'll race you!"

I ran halfway down the pier alongside Lily and Miranda. I didn't allow myself to look back. The August heat wrapped its familiar arms around me and the twinkling lights of the boardwalk brightened the night sky.

Nothing is going to happen, I told myself. The darkness was gone.

Lily's Uncle Paul – who surprisingly wasn't related to her but was a close family friend, so she called him uncle too – found us a table in the corner of his shop, Scoops.

"Look, they left the whipped cream here," I remarked, pointing to the silver can on our pink tabletop. "And sprinkles. And chips."

"That's the cool thing about Scoops," Lily explained. "All the toppings are on the table. You make your own sundae."

"Amazing!" I reached for the bowl of caramel the waitress left for us. I actually like the toppings best. I just use the ice cream as an excuse. I began to pile on whipped cream and caramel. "I love do-it-yourself."

"Ew, what's with the cherries?" Lily squealed. "Check out Miranda."

I looked and my eyes briefly registered the bouquet of maraschino cherries Miranda created by knotting the stems together. I felt my gaze drawn behind her. There stood the old man with the cane. His eyes bore into me.

With a disgusted groan, I wrenched my gaze away.

"I'm not doing anything wrong, you know," Miranda said.

"Huh?" I tried to focus on Miranda, but he kept pulling me towards him.

"I was just having fun." Miranda pushed the cherry bundle onto her napkin. "You don't have to look so grossed-out."

"I'm not." My voice came out in a squeak. I wriggled in my chair, trying desperately to control my body. My fingers found their way into my pocket. The stone. I needed the pink stone.

Sara.

He wanted my attention. My full attention.

Sara . . .

He called to me. My stomach heaved, and the smell of the sugary caramel caused me to gag.

"Gross," Miranda whispered to Lily.

I wanted to turn and see Lily. What was her reaction? But I couldn't. The old man's spirit had invaded my vision.

All I saw was him. His fear. His anguish. And then orange.

The aroma of acrid smoke invaded my nose.

The orange became red then yellow.

Sweat trickled down the back of my shirt as heat spread around me. Within me.

Flames danced before me.

I needed help. I tried to scream but couldn't.

My fingers clawed the cold linoleum of the table.

Suddenly I understood.

The fire was not here. The fire I saw, I smelled, I felt, was happening now – at the haunted house!

CHAPTER 14

I jumped up from the table, sending the bowl of coloured sprinkles skittering across the table in a rainbow explosion.

I couldn't stop to clean it up. I darted around the other customers and bolted out the door.

"Sara!"

Lily's worried call rang out behind me, but I didn't turn back. My flip-flops smacked the boardwalk as I raced towards Midnight Manor.

Would I make it in time? Had the building already burned down?

I passed the fudge shop, and the purple house rose into view. No smell of smoke in the air. No flames. The house looked fine. Normal.

But I didn't stop. I couldn't.

I searched the area for David. Where was he?

Then I spotted him by the side door.

"Is – is there a fire?" My breath came out in ragged gasps. I bent over, hands on my knees as I struggled to calm my pounding heart.

"Say what?" David screwed up his face.

I quickly scanned the building again. I could see it wasn't burning. I could hear Lily and Miranda running up behind me. I knew the smart thing – the normal thing – would be to walk away or turn the whole thing into a joke. But the feeling – it was still with me.

Darkness.

The heat of the invisible flames.

The pull to the house.

I *wasn't* wrong.

I grabbed David's shoulder. I had to make him understand. "Listen, I know I sound all weird. I get that, but you've got to listen to me. Something bad is going to happen here. *Now.* I can't explain how I know it, I just do. Please! Trust me."

David's eyes widened. I'd definitely got his attention.

For what felt like the longest minute ever, he stared

at me intently. He searched my face and looked deeply into my eyes. I guess he saw something that made him believe me.

Then he sprang into action.

He opened the mansion door and hit the main light switch. "Out! Everybody out!" he screamed. He left me to walk through the house.

My brain was spinning. *Fire.* If the house wasn't burning now, would it start soon? Had the old man's spirit been giving me a clue?

I needed to do something, but what? How could I stop a fire?

"Wait, I'm not following," Miranda said. "Why did you make David get those kids out?" She pointed towards the six grumbling kids who were exiting.

"It's not safe," I replied, still trying to untangle the puzzle in my mind.

"What gives you the right to say that?" Miranda challenged.

"Just a feeling," I mumbled.

"What—?"

"Back off, okay?" Lily interrupted Miranda. I could feel her watching me. She didn't seem skeptical, though.

David appeared at my side. "Kids are all out. But seriously, Sara, I'm not seeing anything bad inside. I don't know what you want me to do."

I didn't either. Was someone going to set a fire? Or was something inside the house going to ignite?

I reached into my pocket for the stone. Protection from evil. I needed it now more than ever. My hand touched my camera. I pulled it out, an idea slowly forming. Shading the digital screen with my hand, I scrolled through all the photos I had taken inside Midnight Manor. There had to be something we missed.

Lightbulbs. Dusty window ledges. The chandelier's pulley system. A fake skeleton hand. Mahogany stairs. Mirrors.

The photos revealed nothing out of the ordinary.

And then . . .

I gasped, then pressed the wide-angle button to enlarge the next shot.

"David." My voice came out in a whisper.

A vision of flames flashed before me. The crackling of embers reverberated in my ears. Had I found what I was looking for?

"David," I began again. I raised the screen so he

could see it too. "See all the candles?" The panoramic shot revealed a room filled with dozens of electric candelabras. "How do they light up?"

"Electricity. They're plugged in. Why?"

I could hear my dad. Cautioning me. Telling me the dangers of old houses and their out-of-date wiring. "Are there a lot of sockets?" I asked.

"No, just one. There's an extension cord behind that sofa there that's loaded up."

Now. Help now.

The voice. The old man shimmered to my right. He raised his cane and pointed inside the house.

"Let's look there." I hurried inside with David. He expertly wound his way through the maze-like rooms until we reached the candelabra room. I could feel the old man with us. His fear mixed with mine. My fingers clutched the pink stone.

David heaved the brocade sofa from the wall, exposing a network of tangled extension cords piled with plugs. "Seems okay," he murmured. Then he put his hand to the wall by the lone outlet and let out a quick yelp. "The wall is burning hot!"

He whipped out his phone and dialed 911.

"We need to get out of here now," he said. "Fire trucks are on their way."

Once outside, we heard the approaching sirens. In minutes, firefighters and police officers rushed the building and pushed the growing crowd back.

My mobile phone buzzed from my back pocket. A text from Dad.

Where are u kiddo? Time to be home.

Sorry. On my way.

Want me to walk u?

No. Im good.

I tucked the phone in my pocket, then slid the gemstone, still warm from my grasp, next to it.

I gazed at the house, now alive with activity. Word filtered through the onlookers. The wall had been opened, and the wires inside were smoldering. They were only moments away from sparking into a blaze.

The disaster of a fire had been stopped.

I noticed that the dark feeling had lifted. A calmness came over me. I felt light, free and remarkably alone. The old man's spirit was nowhere in sight.

Neither was Lily, Miranda or David. They were lost in the crowd.

I did it, I realised. I stopped a really bad thing.

My knees wobbled as I thought about it. I needed to be away from the noise to wrap my mind around what just happened. I turned to leave. I'd text Lily later.

"Wait. Sara, wait!" David jogged over to me.

I stopped several yards from the house.

"How did you know?" he asked, looking me straight in the eye.

I looked away and focused my eyes on his worn black canvas sneakers.

"How did you know about the fire?" he asked again.

I raised my gaze to meet his. Should I tell him everything?

CHAPTER 15

"Excuse me. Pardon me. Press," a pretty blonde woman called, pushing through the small crowd. A bearded man with a handheld video camera trailed her. "Anyone here have a comment?"

People eagerly gathered in front of the camera, all sudden experts on building safety.

I examined David's trainers yet again. If I told him – anyone – I'd be the freaky girl on the evening news. There was no way I was doing that.

"I have no idea," I told him, my voice incredulous. "I can't explain it. I just had a really weird feeling."

"You just had a really weird feeling?" David repeated, clearly unsure if he should believe me.

"Yeah." I shrugged. "It's crazy, right?"

"Totally crazy!" Lily bounded over. Her eyes

twinkled with the excitement of the scene. "It's so cool that you had that feeling. I've had feelings like that before too."

"You have?" My heart skipped a beat.

"Oh, totally. I had the strongest feeling in April when our family was together at Easter that my cousin Izzy's boyfriend was going to propose. I got this feeling just by the way he would look at her, you know? And guess what? A month later he did." Lily beamed. "My feeling was so spot-on. Just like yours, Sara."

I was so happy that she had absolutely no idea how I knew about the fire – and didn't seem to care that I did. "Exactly," I said.

David still stared at me.

"Oh, there's my mum and Cammie." Lily motioned somewhere in the distance. "She's probably looking for me. Be right back." She hurried off.

I gnawed my bottom lip, waiting for David to say something. Not sure what to say when he did.

He adjusted the brim of his baseball cap. "Okay," he said slowly. "Whatever." He seemed willing to accept my story. For now.

"My dad's waiting for me," I said, backing away. "I've got to go."

"Hey," he said suddenly, "thanks."

"For?"

"For making me get those kids out. For making me listen to your . . . feeling."

"You're welcome." I smiled widely. I wondered what he'd think if he knew my feeling had a face, a body, could speak . . . and had been dead almost fifty years!

I sifted through a handful of sea glass from the pile beside me. Sitting cross-legged on the front porch, I arranged them carefully around the photos of the pier, the lighthouse and the beach I'd decoupaged onto the wooden tray.

"That boy at Midnight Manor is certainly a hero," my dad remarked. His face was hidden behind the local paper.

"It says that?"

"Yep. Big article." He paused for a gulp of coffee, quickly reading to the end. "He evacuated the haunted house and summoned the fire department, all before any flames broke out. Amazing, really. I mean, think about the property damage he avoided, not to mention the lives he saved."

From his white wicker chair, he peered over the paper at me. "It was an overloaded circuit. A wiring issue. Didn't I tell you about that?"

"You did."

"Good morning, all." Lady Azura glided onto the front porch in a swirl of ivory chiffon.

I was surprised to see her this early. She usually took hours "putting on her face," as she called it. I rarely saw her before noon. Today she was already made-up.

"Big doings at the pier last night, I hear," she remarked. She perched on the swing, giving the knitting spirit plenty of room. "Wonderful when things work out as they should." Her red lips raised in the slightest smile.

"You're friends with that boy, aren't you?" Dad asked me. He stood, put down his coffee mug and paper, and got ready to leave for the office.

"Kind of, I guess."

"Well, you should be very proud of him. Not

many kids get involved today. It's good to see someone do something good."

"I am proud," I said quietly. I was proud of David. And, I realised, I was proud of me.

That was because of me, I thought. The old man came to me for help. I was the one who could hear him. I was the one who figured it out. Maybe this was what it was all about. Helping people.

Maybe seeing spirits was okay.

"So what's the plan today, kiddo?" Dad asked. "Back to the pier?"

I shook my head. "Lily invited me over. She and her mum have this plan to teach themselves to make a blueberry pie. I'm going to help."

"Sounds tasty. Lily and you are getting to be friends?" His voice had that hopeful ring.

"Yeah. I think we are." Lily and I had texted for a long time last night. She didn't press me about what happened at Midnight Manor. She'd just gone with it. I had the feeling that was the way she was.

"Save me a piece of pie." Dad waved as he headed down the front walk.

"I think it was kind of meant for you, anyway.

A belated welcome," I explained. I thought about the last couple of weeks. "But I'm not feeling as new anymore."

Dad beamed as he drove off.

I turned my attention back to the tray. Using a toothpick, I dabbed glue on the sea glass. The *click-clack* of the spirit's knitting needles mingled with the intermittent cries of the seagulls. Upstairs I could hear the faint rocking of the sad woman's chair. They had become the sounds of home.

Lady Azura watched me silently. "You are happier now."

I thought about it. "I guess I am."

"It's good to be involved," she stated simply.

What does she mean? I wondered. *Does she know what I did at the haunted house?* I lowered my eyes and positioned the green glass next to the blue.

"Do you have something you want to tell me, Sara?" she asked.

I gulped. She must know about George. I sort of wanted to share everything with her . . . and I sort of didn't. I was scared. Would she truly understand?

"Sara." Her voice was insistent.

I raised my eyes. "Well, I—" I stopped when I noticed her outstretched hand.

"I know you took my gemstone, Sara. It wasn't yours to take."

My face grew red and hot. "I'm sorry." I reached into my shorts pocket and pulled out the pink stone. "I'm not like that. Really, I'm not. I just saw it, and you said it protects from evil, and it called to me like you said." I bit my lip to keep from babbling. I dropped the gemstone in her wrinkled palm.

"I'm sorry." I said again.

She turned the stone around in her palm, examining it. "I know the allure of beautiful things. But next time, ask."

I nodded vigorously. I was so embarrassed.

"Did it work? Did it protect you?"

I recalled the warmth of the smooth stone spreading across my hand when George's spirit pulled at me. "It did."

She thought about this. "Interesting, considering you took the wrong stone." She held the stone close to her eyes. "This stone is rhodonite, not tourmaline. It is used to strengthen our resolve."

"What's that mean?"

"It's that little nudge to do what we already know we can do. A belief in our abilities. Courage." She stood. "Follow me."

I trailed after her into the house and through the purple velvet curtain. At the shelves lined with stones and crystals, she replaced the one I took. She surveyed first the shelves and then me. "Protection is not what you need at this time."

"What do I need?"

She selected a ruby crystal and raised it in the dim light. "This will encourage love to bloom and grow."

"Love?" The word came out in a funny snort.

"Ahh, yes, child, it is time for love." She reached once more for my palm. "School will be starting soon. As I told you and I see plainly here"—she pointed to a short line near my ring finger— "you will meet a tall, dark stranger."

I couldn't help it. I laughed. Quickly, I tried to cover my mouth with my hands. *Why do I keep thinking she has powers?* I scolded myself. I have to stop.

Gently, she closed my fingers around the crystal,

then covered my hand with both her hands. Her grasp was warm. Not sweaty, but hot. An intense heat pulsed from her to me. A staticky sensation tickled my nerves. The edges of my vision grew blurry, then clouded over. I wanted to pull away from her, but my legs felt weak.

Then through the haze I saw him.

His dark hair fell long over his forehead. Tall and athletic-looking, he had piercing eyes, a straight nose and a warm grin. He leaned against a school locker and helped a girl with her books. The girl turned to him, and they shared a secret smile.

I gasped when I saw her face.

The girl was me!

In an instant, the vision was gone. I wasn't in school. I was standing in Lady Azura's room, the crystal pressed against my palm. I wrenched away from her, my heart pounding.

What had I just seen?

And what did it all mean?

Want to know what happens to Sara next?

Here's a sneak peek at the next book in the series:

HAUNTED MEMORIES

No one saw me.

I pressed my back against the pale-green cafeteria wall. How long would it be before anyone noticed I existed? Minutes? Hours? Days? The entire school year?

Yesterday was different. Everyone smiled. New clothes. New haircuts. New binders. Blank paper organised perfectly into labelled sections. Even teachers smiled, swept up in the great-to-be-back vibe.

There were a lot fewer smiles today. The second day.

By now Stellamar Middle School was old news to everyone – except me. I gnawed my bottom lip, pretended to smooth wrinkles on my favourite sky-blue top, and scanned the cafeteria.

I don't belong here. I'm not one of them, I thought.

Can they see I'm different? Can they sense it? I choked back a laugh. *Seriously, Sara. Stop being silly,* I scolded myself. *No one senses anything. They don't even notice you.*

Yesterday I spent lunch in the guidance office as they sorted out my records from my old school. I wondered if I should head back there. Create another problem for them to solve.

"Oh, wow! Can you believe Mrs Moyers kept me after class? Like I really need a reminder not to speak without raising my hand. Come on, we're in seventh grade." Lily Randazzo rushed through the cafeteria door. She scooped her arm through mine and propelled me into the lunchroom. I hurried to keep up as she expertly wove her way around kids wandering aimlessly with plastic lunch trays. "You don't have her, do you?" Lily continued, not stopping to say hi or even breathe. "I wish we had more classes together. But you like it here, right? All's good, right?"

"Sure." I wasn't sure, but I didn't know what else to say. At the moment, I was just grateful to be wrapped in the whirlwind of Lily.

"There's barely any time to eat," Lily announced to a

long table filled with girls. "Scoot down, Avery, okay?"

"Sure thing." Avery smiled, showing off a rainbow of rubber bands on her braces.

"Can you push down for Sara, too?" Lily asked. "She just moved to my street this summer. Everyone, this is Sara." Lily pointed to me.

My face grew warm as the girls stopped eating and stared. I wasn't like Lily, who loved attention. I was happier on the edge of a crowd. But I liked Lily, and I wanted her friends to like me. "Hi," I managed. My voice sounded unnaturally squeaky.

I quickly slid onto the bench next to Lily. Avery leaned across Lily's sandwich and squinted at me with slate-grey eyes. "You're really pretty," she said finally. From the way she said it, I wasn't sure if it was a compliment or an accusation.

"Oh . . . thanks." I pulled out my container of mixed-berry yogurt and tried to be friendly. "I like your braces."

"I decided to go all Roy G. Biv. You know, the total rainbow." Avery flashed a full-tooth grin. She had a different colour rubber band on each tooth.

"Sara looks like that because she's from California," Miranda announced. She sat across from Avery.

I'd met Miranda a few weeks ago on the board-walk with Lily, but I didn't know her well.

"That makes no sense, Miranda," scoffed a thin girl with wavy, reddish hair. "There's no way everyone in California is, like, that pretty."

All the girls stared at me again. I didn't know what to say. I didn't want to talk about how I looked.

"That's true. There are ugly people in California too," Lily piped in. "But Sara looks like a surfer girl. I mean, wouldn't you cast her in one of those sunscreen adverts? She'd be great in that new one with that girl on the paddleboard."

"Why did you move to New Jersey?" Avery asked.

"My father got a new job," I explained, relieved at the change in subject. I told them a little about his job and our move. I didn't tell them that he'd been fired from his old job or that his girlfriend had dumped him. I didn't tell them that I still couldn't figure out why we had to suddenly move across the country when life seemed perfectly okay in California.

But I was used to keeping information to myself.